THE

Special two-in-one edition

Treasure Hunt
The Empty House

The Mystery Kids series

THE MYSTERY KIDS
Treasure Hunt

Fiona Kelly

Hodder
Children's
Books

a division of Hodder Headline plc

*This volume of Treasure Hunt and The Empty House
first published in Great Britain in 1997
ISBN 0 340 70879 4*

Treasure Hunt
Special thanks to Michael Coleman

Copyright © 1995 Ben Baglio
Created by Ben M. Baglio
London W6 0HE

First published in Great Britain in 1995
by Hodder Children's Books

A Catalogue record for this book is
available from the British Library

Typeset by Avon Dataset Ltd, Bidford-on-Avon, Warks
Printed and bound in Great Britain by
Mackays of Chatham PLC, Chatham, Kent

Hodder Children's Books
a division of Hodder Headline plc
338 Euston Road
London NW1 3BH

Contents

An unsolved puzzle

'Knock, knock.'

Holly Adams screwed up her nose, closed her eyes, and pretended not to hear. There were times for bad jokes and, as far as she was concerned, this wasn't one of them.

'Come on, come on,' said her best friend, Miranda Hunt, from the other side of the room. 'Knock, knock.'

Holly looked up. She knew she couldn't win. When Miranda was testing jokes for *The Tom-tom*, the lower-school magazine, nothing could stop her. 'Who's there?' she sighed.

'Isadora.'

'Isadora who?'

'Isadora open arounda here? I'm freezing!'

In spite of herself, Holly smiled. 'Miranda, that's terrible.'

'You really think so?'

1

'No,' said Holly. 'I was just being polite. Really, I think it's worse than terrible.'

'Good,' said Miranda. 'It's definitely in then.'

She bent low over the sheet of paper on the coffee table, her corn-coloured hair flopping into her eyes as she wrote. She sat back with a grin. 'Right, that's the jokes column done. How are you getting on, Holly?'

'I'm not,' said Holly.

'How come?'

'Maybe because I keep getting interrupted by someone testing bad jokes on me.'

'Well, they've got to be tested on someone, haven't they?' said Miranda. 'Our magazine has to keep its standards up.'

'Or down, where your jokes are concerned.'

Miranda laughed. It wasn't one of her loudest laughs – they, in Holly's view, would qualify for a place in the *Guinness Book of Records* section on loud noises – but a fairly gentle laugh, doing no more than make the windows rattle.

'So, how *is* the mystery column getting on?' she said.

Holly slumped back in her armchair and

pointed to the blank sheet of paper in front of her. 'There you are. That's it!'

'Oh dear,' said Miranda. 'No ideas?'

Holly shook her head. She'd never had this trouble before.

'Maybe it was a bad idea to try to put together an issue of the magazine for the first week of term,' she said.

'No it wasn't,' said Miranda. 'It was a great idea.'

'You think so?'

'I *know* so.' She waved a hand around the Adams's lounge. 'For one thing your house is more comfortable than the resources room at school . . .'

'Is that all?'

'Of course it isn't. You know what it's like when we go back to school after the holidays – everybody has a face as long as a wet weekend. But with a first-week issue of the magazine in their hands, just think how much happier they'll be!'

'Even with your jokes in it?'

'Especially with my jokes in it! Now, what's the problem with the mystery column?'

'Nothing's happening. Nothing at all.'

3

The idea of the mystery column was to report on the latest mystery books, or on mystery series showing on television. Usually it was a case of Holly having to decide what to leave out. But not today.

'I haven't seen a single new mystery book in the shops,' continued Holly, 'and absolutely everything on television is a repeat. They're even showing *The Man From U.N.C.L.E.* again!'

'I know,' said Miranda. 'My dad says they were repeats when *he* was a kid!'

Holly got to her feet and began to pace up and down. 'What we need,' she said thoughtfully, 'is something *new*.'

'Like my jokes, you mean?' said Miranda.

'*Not* like your jokes,' began Holly. 'My dad says most of your jokes are old enough to have been taken on board by Noah . . .' She stopped, her eyes brightening as an idea came to her. 'Hey! Wait a minute. Why not?' She started pacing up and down the lounge again. 'Yes, why not . . .'

'Excuse me, can anybody join this conversation?' said Miranda. 'Why not what?'

'Why not,' Holly said enthusiastically, 'an *old* mystery? Maybe . . .'

4

'Maybe, maybe?'

'Maybe one that's *never* been solved!'

Miranda nodded approvingly. 'I like it! Hey – how about Jack the Ripper?'

Holly wrinkled her nose. 'For the lower-school magazine?'

'Hmm, perhaps not,' said Miranda.

'But that sort of thing, definitely,' said Holly. She thought a bit more. 'Or maybe even a legend.'

'You mean, something that might or might not be true? Like . . .' Miranda clicked her fingers as she searched for a good example. 'Like King Arthur and Camelot and all that lot?'

'No. Not exactly.'

'Yes, you're probably right,' sniffed Miranda. She gave a sudden laugh, 'Hey! I've just thought – why was Camelot the dumbest place?'

'Huh?'

'Because it was ruled by King Arthur and the Nits of the Round Table!'

'Miranda!' laughed Holly. But she'd got the point. 'OK, forget the legend idea. But an article about an unsolved mystery – that could be really good.'

5

She was still thinking as she drifted out to the kitchen to make another round of milk-shakes. Holly's mother and father both worked during the day, her father as a solicitor and her mother as the assistant manager of a bank. Holly couldn't say she liked the arrangement, but it did mean she could make milk-shakes to her heart's content. She'd just stuck her head into the fridge when the front doorbell rang.

'Miranda!' yelled Holly. 'Could you see who it is, please? And what flavour do you want – strawberry again?'

'Yes, please,' said Miranda as she went to the front door. Then, moments later, she called, 'And chocolate for the paper boy.'

For the paper boy? What is Miranda doing, thought Holly. *Inviting the whole street in for drinks?*

She popped her head out of the kitchen door, just in time to see Miranda returning from the front door followed by a tall, skinny boy with a newspaper bag looped over his shoulder.

'Peter!' said Holly. 'You didn't say you were coming round.'

Peter Hamilton brushed his hair out of his

eyes with one hand, and patted the paper bag with the other.

'I didn't know I'd be delivering the evening papers.'

'*Evening* papers?' said Miranda. She looked at her watch. 'It's only half-past four.'

'They call it the evening edition,' said Peter – the third member of the Mystery Kids. 'Actually there's another edition later in the day, but we don't deliver it.'

Peter smiled. He looked pleased with himself. 'One of the afternoon boys has gone away for the next two weeks, so I'm doing his round as well as my own. It means,' he said excitedly, 'that taking into account what I've saved so far, by the end of this week . . .' He paused to look at Holly, then at Miranda, and then back at Holly again. '. . . I'll have enough money!'

Holly groaned. It had not been a good afternoon. First it had been Miranda's jokes. Then her own lack of ideas for the mystery column. And now Peter's secret. He had been plaguing them with it all through the holidays.

Peter had first said he was saving up for something at the start of the holidays, explaining that he'd taken on a paper round especially for the purpose. But exactly *what* he was saving up for, he wouldn't say.

Since then, Holly and Miranda had tried everything they knew to get him to say what it was. They'd tried persuasion. They'd tried pretending they didn't care (which they certainly did!). Once Holly had said that she would set Jamie on to him, but even the threat of being interrogated by Holly's gruesome little brother hadn't budged Peter's resolve. His secret was still secret.

Once more, she told herself. She'd try once more. 'Have enough money for what, Peter?'

But Peter just smiled. 'I can't tell you – in case they're gone when I get there. But they were there the last time I looked.'

'You want a mystery, Holly?' said Miranda. 'Meet Peter Hamilton, a boy who is a complete mystery!'

Peter laughed, but still said nothing.

Miranda put her hands on Peter's shoulders. 'Peter,' she said sweetly, 'are we, or are we not, the Mystery Kids?'

'Yes, but—'

'Solving mysteries wherever we find them,' said Holly. 'Together.'

'All for one . . .' said Miranda.

'And one for all,' said Holly.

'Yes, but—'

'So secrets between the Mystery Kids are out,' said Miranda softly. 'Agreed?'

Peter nodded. 'Agreed. No secrets.'

'There you are, then!' Miranda said triumphantly.

'And as soon as I get them, I'll tell you. But, if I were to tell you now and then didn't manage to get them, it would be even worse. I'd feel as though I'd let you both down. That would be awful, wouldn't it?'

'It can't be more awful than not knowing what you're on about, can it?' yelled Miranda.

'You'll see,' said Peter. 'All I can say is, they're just what the Mystery Kids need.'

With an exasperated sigh, Holly took the newspaper that Peter was holding and flopped down into an armchair.

'Hey, don't crumple that paper up,' said Peter. 'It's for number seventy-four. You don't have an evening paper from Harry's One-Stop.'

'Then why did you bring us one?' said Holly, rifling through the pages.

'I didn't. I just called in to say hello.'

'Hello,' said Miranda, still miffed. 'Say hello to Peter, Holly.'

'Hello,' Holly said absently.

'Well, that *was* nice wasn't it?' said Miranda. She put her hand in the middle of Peter's back and pushed gently. 'Cheerio, Peter. Do call again.'

'OK, I get the message. But that newspaper . . .'

'Is for number seventy-four,' said Miranda. 'Don't worry, Peter. I'll deliver it for you on my way home.' She looked across at Holly, still with her head in the newspaper. 'If I ever get to go home, that is.'

Peter looked at her questioningly. *'The Tom-tom,'* explained Miranda. 'We've been trying to put an issue together for next week, but there's still a big hole where the mystery column is supposed to be.'

Holly looked up. 'We thought we'd have something about an unsolved mystery. Any ideas?'

'Holly,' said Miranda in mock horror. 'You're asking Peter for ideas? You must be desperate!'

Peter shook his head. 'Not really . . .'

10

'There you are,' said Miranda.

'Unless there's anything on page fifteen,' said Peter, pointing to the newspaper Holly was still flicking through. 'Bottom corner. I haven't had a chance to look at it myself yet.'

Mystified, Holly turned to page fifteen. 'What am I supposed to be looking for?'

'They have a little section on what happened years ago today. Fifty years, twenty-five years—'

He was stopped in his tracks by Holly's shout. Eyes open wide as she looked at the page, she yelled, 'Hey! This could be it!'

As Peter and Miranda gathered round to look, Holly spread the newspaper out on the coffee table. 'Look, look. There!'

' "Ten years ago today . . ." ' Miranda began to read. 'Is that all?'

Holly tapped excitedly at the page with her finger. 'Of course it isn't! Look!'

' ". . . blackmailer Ginger Kane . . ." ' read Peter.

'I couldn't see *that* bit,' said Miranda. 'You had your finger on it.' She bent down to look at the next part of the paragraph, as Peter continued reading.

' ". . . got away with a ransom haul of fifty thousand pounds that had been left in a telephone booth outside Highgate station." '

As he gave a low whistle, Miranda seized her chance to read the next bit.

' "But twenty-five minutes later, Kane was arrested by an off-duty policeman, PC Alan Jenkins, who spotted him and gave chase." Twenty-five minutes later!' exclaimed Miranda. 'Well, *that's* not much of a mystery, is it?'

'No,' said Holly. 'But *this* is.'

She pointed again at the page. There was a simple, final sentence to the paragraph that Miranda hadn't seen.

' "But, by then, Kane had got rid of the money. It has never been found." '

Holly looked at Peter. Peter looked at Miranda. Miranda looked at Holly. They all nodded together.

'Now *there's* a mystery!'

A reference project

'Holly, don't think I'm changing my mind, but . . .'

'But you're changing your mind.'

'No, I'm not,' said Miranda. She swerved across to inspect a pair of boots in a shoe-shop window, then back to Holly without stopping. 'I just don't see how you think we can solve a mystery that's ten years old.'

'I'm not saying we can *solve* it, Miranda,' said Holly. 'Just find out as much about it as we can before term starts. Then I'll write it up for the mystery column.'

The smell of doughnuts wafted out from a baker's shop. Miranda slowed, then hurried to catch up as Holly strode on. 'I take it you're not feeling hungry, then?'

'Miranda, we've just had lunch!'

'We have?'

'At the supermarket?' prompted Holly.

13

'After doing my mum's shopping? That's why we couldn't do this earlier – remember?'

'Of course I remember.' She drew alongside Holly. 'You haven't got anything in your bag, then?'

Holly switched her hold-all from the hand nearest Miranda to the hand furthest away. 'No, I haven't. Well . . . only a couple of cans and some chocolate bars. And they're for afterwards,' she said, switching her hold-all back again as Miranda moved to her other side.

'After we've found out enough for your mystery column? That could take *days*. I could be as pale as a shadow by then.'

Holly laughed. 'You? I don't think so, Miranda.'

They turned a corner. In front of them, at the head of a wide flight of steps, was a large grey building. Even from where they were, they could clearly read the words 'Central Library' carved in the stonework above the entrance.

'So, what sort of information are we looking for?' Miranda asked as they walked towards the library building.

14

'Anything. Everything. What happened. But especially the route. That's what I really want to know something about.'

'The route. What route?'

'Ginger Kane's route. That little bit in yesterday's newspaper said he was captured twenty-five minutes after the alarm was raised. But in that time he managed to hide a case full of money. So where did he go?'

Miranda stopped, her foot poised on the bottom step of the flight leading up to the library entrance.

'Holly, you're not suggesting we try to *look* for that money?'

'Miranda, what sort of idiot do you take me for? I'm not suggesting that we could find something the police haven't found in ten years. But I have had an idea.'

'Another one? Two in two days?'

'Listen. We could run a mystery column competition!'

'Competition? What sort of competition – Spot the Crook?'

'In a way, yes,' said Holly.

'Huh?'

'We write up all we find out about the Ginger Kane story and include a map of the area, showing the route he took. Then we have a competition for our readers to put an "X" on the map showing where they think the money was hidden!'

'Holly, that's brilliant!' cried Miranda.

'We could have winner's and runner-up's prizes.'

'Right! We could give the winner a free copy of the magazine for the rest of the year.'

'How about the runner-up?'

'*Two* free copies of the magazine?'

'Miranda!'

'Only joking,' said Miranda. 'If we *can* find out something about this it will be the best mystery column ever!'

But Holly was already bounding up the flight of steps and pushing through the revolving door which led into the library.

'Upstairs,' Holly said quietly, pointing to a sign marked 'Reference Section, First Floor'.

'I hope they do keep old newspapers in here,' said Miranda, puffing slightly as they went up the stairs. 'Did you think to check?'

'Peter says they do,' said Holly.

'Oh, well,' said Miranda, 'that's all right

then. If the Newspaper Delivery Operative of the Year says they keep them here, then it must be so.'

As they reached the first floor, Holly wondered if the reference section was actually open for business, it was so quiet. She looked round. A few people were sitting at tables in the middle of the area, silently leafing through large books. A couple were taking notes. A man sneezed, and everybody turned to look at him. Holly wondered if Miranda would be able to survive for long without speaking.

She couldn't. 'Where do we start looking?' said Miranda, much too loudly.

'Over there by the looks of it,' said Holly. A pair of eyes were peering at them from behind a semi-circular desk piled high with books and magazines.

Holly led the way over to the desk. A stencilled sign was perched on the front: 'Reference Librarian – Vera Whittle'. The owner of the peering eyes, presumably Vera Whittle herself, stood up.

'Can I help you?' she said in a hushed voice.

Holly looked at Miranda. 'We – we're

after some – well, information,' began Holly.

'Reference information,' Miranda added helpfully.

'Well, you've come to the right place,' said the librarian with a thin smile. 'What sort of reference information?'

'A newspaper,' said Holly. 'The *Highgate Herald*.'

The librarian pointed over towards a pair of pyramid-shaped racks. 'Today's newspapers are over there,' she said. 'National papers on the left, local papers on the right.'

'Oh. No, thanks – but we don't want to look at today's newspapers.'

'Yesterday's are there, too,' said the librarian. 'I don't store them until they're two days old.'

'You do store them, then?'

'Of course,' sighed the librarian. 'This is a *reference* library, dear.'

'Great!' Miranda said brightly. 'Because that's what she wants, don't you, Holly? To look at an *old Highgate Herald*.'

'How old?'

'Absolutely *ages* old,' said Miranda.

'From ten years ago,' said Holly. 'It's – it's

for a school project we're doing,' she added. For a moment she wondered whether she'd told a lie, then realised she hadn't. It was quite true – the magazine *was* a school project.

The librarian's eyebrows shot up. A faint smile flickered across her face. 'Oh. How nice to see young people interested in the past. But ten years ago . . .'

'You do keep them for that long, don't you?' said Miranda. 'This being a *reference* library and all that.'

'Yes, we do,' said the librarian. 'But newspapers take a lot of space. So most of them are kept in our stack.'

'Stack?'

'Storeroom,' said the librarian. 'Along with the old books. Can you come back on Monday?'

Holly couldn't hide her disappointment. 'Monday? Not today?'

'Stack retrievals take time, dear,' said the librarian. 'I would have to make a special trip to get the newspaper you want.' She waved a hand over the pile of books and magazines on her desk. 'And I've so much work to do I really haven't got time to go again just now.'

She picked up a ball-point pen with her name sellotaped round the stem. 'So, which date are you interested in?'

Holly paused before answering. If it meant going through a performance like this every time, she wanted to be sure that she asked the librarian for the right one.

'Can I look at more than one?'

'*Highgate Herald*s are stored by the week,' said the librarian. 'Six newspapers, Monday to Saturday.' She waited, her pen in the air.

Holly searched through her hold-all and pulled out her notebook. She'd copied out the snippet they'd seen in yesterday's paper. The chase had taken place on Wednesday 26th August, ten years earlier. So she wanted the bundle for that week.

'Week commencing Monday 24th of August,' she said.

The librarian looked up. 'August? You did say August?'

'Please,' said Holly.

The librarian was frowning. Suddenly she slipped from her chair and knelt down on the floor.

'You shouldn't have said "please",' whispered Miranda. 'She's fainted!'

Holly looked over the desk. The librarian hadn't fainted. She was busy shuffling through a shelf under the desk. When she stood up again, she had a small pile of newspapers in her arms.

'*Highgate Herald* for the week commencing Monday 24th August,' she said. Her lips tweaked at the corners in a half-smile as Holly gasped in amazement.

'Really?'

'Yes, really,' said the librarian. She pointed towards a row of glass-panelled booths on the far side of the floor. 'Booth two is free. I suggest you look through them in there.'

Holly took the newspapers. 'Thanks.'

'Very good,' said Miranda. 'Very good indeed. Most impressive.'

'You just happened to be lucky,' said the librarian. 'They were the newspapers I went to get from the stack earlier today. I just haven't had time to put them back yet.'

'Well, thanks anyway,' said Holly, struggling with her notebook, her hold-all and the newspapers. 'Over there did you say?'

'Number two,' said Miranda. She took Holly's hold-all. "Let's go. You carry the papers, I'll carry the chocolate and drinks.'

'Not in here, you don't.' It was Vera Whittle, looking serious again. 'No eating. No drinking. This is a library, not a cafeteria.'

'A *reference* library,' Miranda muttered as they crossed the floor. 'Oh come on, Holly, let's get on with it. I'm dying of thirst!'

They pushed open the door to the study booth. It was small and cosy, with just a table and two chairs.

'She's not watching us,' said Miranda, looking out to where the librarian had gone back to sorting through the papers on her desk. 'Let's get the cans out, Holly.'

She began to unload Holly's hold-all. Out came the cans of drink, the chocolate bars – and a magnifying glass.

'What's this for?'

'I thought it might come in useful,' said Holly.

'What for, reading the small print?'

'Are we supposed to be investigators or not?' said Holly. She took the magnifying glass from Miranda and laid it carefully on the table.

Miranda thought for a moment, then nodded. 'We are.' She grinned. 'And the first thing I'm going to investigate is one of those cans.'

'No, you're not,' Holly said as Miranda reached across the table.

'Why ever not?'

Holly nodded her head towards the glass panel. 'Because you-know-who is watching.'

Miranda turned round and saw that Vera Whittle was indeed looking straight at them.

'Crafty devil! No wonder she sent us to this one. It's the only study booth she can see straight into!'

With a sigh, Miranda turned to the newspapers Holly had begun to spread out on the table. 'Bit of luck these being around, wasn't it?'

'Was it?' said Holly.

'What else do you call it?' said Miranda, leaning back so that her chair was balancing on its rear legs.

'Suspicious,' said Holly. 'That's what I call it.' She looked at her friend. 'Two people asking for the same papers on the same day?'

'Some coincidence, huh?' said Miranda.

'Papers that are ten years old? Miranda, that's an awfully big coincidence.'

Miranda let her chair fall forward with a thump. 'Of course!'

'Shh!' hissed Holly. Through the glass panel she could see the librarian glaring in their direction.

Miranda looked round, smiled sweetly in the librarian's direction, then turned back again. 'Of course,' she whispered dramatically. 'It's obvious!'

'What's obvious?'

'Call yourself a Mystery Kid, Holly Adams? Use your brain. Who else knew what we were looking for?'

'Peter?'

'Who else?'

It was a good question. Now that it had been suggested to her, Holly couldn't think of anybody else.

'That was kind of him,' said Holly. 'Trying to help.'

'Trying to help? Trying to get here first, more like!' exclaimed Miranda.

'Peter? Why?'

'I don't know,' said Miranda. 'To get his own back, I suppose. Just because we didn't show any interest in his big secret.'

'But we *did* show an interest in his secret,

Miranda. We were dying to find out what he was planning to buy, you know we were.'

'True,' said Miranda. 'Then he's probably tried to beat us to it because we were *too* interested. Boys are like that. You don't know what's going on between their ears.'

'Hmm, maybe,' said Holly. 'Well, let's see what we can find out for ourselves while we're here.'

She picked up the newspaper for Monday, 24th August and laid it aside. She did the same for the paper dated the following day. 'This one,' she said, picking up the next paper in the pile.

'Wednesday, the 26th of August,' said Miranda, scanning the front page. 'Just think. All this happened when I was a teeny-weeny baby.'

'And I bet you were as much of a pain then as you are now,' laughed Holly. She turned over to page two.

'Wouldn't it have been on the front page?' said Miranda. 'A big story like that?'

Holly nodded thoughtfully. 'I would have thought so.' Something that had been said the day before came back to her. 'Maybe this was an early edition for that day. Didn't Peter say that they print more than one edition per day?'

'Something like that. I switch off whenever Peter starts to explain boring things like that.'

Holly flipped over the final page. 'Nothing. The story must have been too late to get in the paper for August the 26th; it must be in Thursday's paper.'

Miranda swept up the top paper from the pile left on the table. 'Good thinking. It must be this one. No,' she said, putting it down again. 'This is Friday the 28th.'

'And this is Saturday the 29th,' said Holly, picking up the remaining newspaper on the table.

She looked at her friend. 'Miranda, it's missing!'

3 Mystery headline

'You don't think Peter's stolen it?' said Miranda.

Holly shrugged. 'Well, it isn't here . . .'

She looked through the pile again. Monday, Tuesday, Wednesday, Friday, Saturday. But no Thursday. Then she noticed that Friday's edition looked thicker than the others. She peeled open the centre pages of Friday's edition – and there it was. The *Highgate Herald* crest and, above it, the date: Thursday 27th August.

'Good old Peter,' Miranda said as she saw it. 'Can't even stack a few newspapers without getting them mixed up. What on earth's he like on that paper round of his!'

She looked at Holly. 'Hey. What's up?'

'Look,' Holly said simply. 'It wasn't put in there by accident. It was hidden.'

Then Miranda saw why. Apart from the

newspaper's crest, there was hardly anything left of the front page. Most of it had been ripped out.

'That's torn it,' said Miranda. 'Sorry, that wasn't meant to be a joke. It's not funny.'

'No, it isn't,' said Holly. 'Surely Peter wouldn't do this?'

'Who else could it have been?' said Miranda. 'It must have been whoever came here before us, otherwise they would have mentioned it to Eagle-eyes Vera out there. It must have been Peter.'

'I suppose so.' Holly snapped open her notebook angrily. 'It's not right. OK, so tearing the page out was quicker than copying down the details. But it's vandalism. Somebody else might want to look at this paper.'

'Somebody else *did* want to look at this paper,' said Miranda. 'Us! Now look at it. The thing looks like it's been attacked by a runaway shredder.'

The page had been torn out violently, the top corner crumpled as though it had been held in one hand while the rest of the page was being torn out with the other. 'He did it in a hurry,' said Holly. 'He was scared of being caught.'

Miranda glanced out to where the librarian was still sitting. 'Who wouldn't be?' She turned back.

Holly looked closer at the torn page. 'And it was done by a right-handed person. Peter's right-handed . . .'

Miranda blinked. 'Hang on. I've missed a bit. How'd you work that one out?'

'It's been torn from right to left, see? You can only do that if you hold it down with your left hand while you tear it with your right.'

'What if he turned it upside down?' said Miranda.

'Hmm. I hadn't thought of that.' Holly looked down at the ruined front page.

'Anyway, knowing that the culprit is right-handed doesn't narrow it down much!' said Miranda.

'Well, right- or left-handed, he's not left much, has he?' said Holly, annoyed.

Under the newspaper's title, all that remained of the front page was a fragment of a headline and an almost-complete photograph of a man.

Holly picked up her magnifying glass and peered through it. 'Do you think he's one of them?'

'Definitely,' said Miranda, moving round to look over her shoulder. 'I mean, look at him. If he's not a crook I'd like to see the picture of somebody who is. Talk about shifty-looking.'

'It doesn't say who it is,' said Holly. 'The caption must be on the part that was torn out.'

Miranda gave the face another close look. The man was thin on top, and looked as if he had recently been in a fight. A short row of stitches ran across his left cheekbone. 'It's got to be Ginger Kane,' Miranda said firmly. 'It can't be anybody else. He probably got that cut resisting arrest.'

'His eyebrows meet in the middle. Isn't that a bad sign?'

'It certainly is! And look at those eyes, Holly!' Miranda moved the magnifying glass out so that the eyes in the photograph expanded like balloons. 'A *blackmailer*'s eyes if ever I saw them.'

Holly looked at her friend with a smile. 'Why, what do a blackmailer's eyes look like?'

'Those!' said Miranda, tapping the picture sharply. She gazed at the remains of the page. 'Not much else though, is there?'

As Holly had said, the page had been torn from right to left. Only a ragged triangular section was left, and most of this was taken up by the photograph. Of the rest, only part of the headline was visible:

Chase ends in Pol

'Chase ends in Pol?' said Holly. 'What would that have been?'

Miranda made a face. ' "Chase ends in Polly the Parrot's cage!" ' She gave a laugh that rattled the windows.

'Sh!' said Holly. Outside the booth, heads rose and the librarian glared daggers in their direction.

Holly looked at the headline again. 'I expect it was something about being chased by the police. "Chase ends in police arrest" or something like that.'

'Hmm, you're probably right,' said Miranda.

'Well, we'll find out when we see Peter. Come on, let's go before you get us thrown out.' Holly folded up the torn newspaper.

As she finished, Miranda took it from her and carefully put it back where they'd found it, hidden inside the Friday edition.

'What are you doing that for?'

'Why do you think?' whispered Miranda. 'Do you want Vera the Vampire to charge us with newspaper vandalism? That would make a good headline, wouldn't it? "Mystery Kid turns into Holly the Ripper." '

'I suppose you're right,' said Holly.

With the Friday edition at the bottom of the pile, they left the study booth and tiptoed back to the librarian's desk.

'Find what you were looking for?' Vera Whittle asked frostily. She gave them a look which clearly said that this part of the library was strictly a laughter-free zone.

'Yes, thank you,' said Holly. Her heart was pounding. They hadn't done anything wrong, and yet she still felt guilty.

'Thank you,' she said again as she handed the newspapers over.

'Sorry about the noise,' added Miranda. She held a hand to her throat and gave a little cough. 'Sore throat.'

The two girls started towards the door. Would they make it? They started walking away. Then they heard the librarian's voice.

'Just a minute.'

Holly's heart missed a beat. The torn

pages. They were in trouble. Slowly, she and Miranda turned round. She knew what was coming. The librarian would be holding up the remnants of the page with the photograph on it . . .

But she wasn't. She had a wintry smile on her face and was holding out something towards Miranda. A tin of cough sweets!

'Have one of these. It might help.'

With a gurgled 'Thanks very much', Miranda took a sweet from Vera Whittle's tin and stuffed it in her mouth.

'And no running!' the librarian called as they disappeared through the door.

4 Who, me?

Holly strode determinedly up the stairway leading to the flat Peter lived in with his father. It was Monday afternoon.

Behind her, Miranda was having trouble keeping up. 'He's probably not in again,' she called. They'd tried once on Sunday and again that morning.

'He's probably out paper-rounding or whatever they call it,' puffed Miranda. 'I don't know why you don't want to phone him.'

'Because I want to talk to him face-to-face,' said Holly. She checked her watch. Two o'clock. 'And he shouldn't be out yet. His afternoon round doesn't start until half-past four. He said so on Friday.'

As they reached the second-floor landing, she pushed through the swing doors.

'I bet he'll have a good excuse,' said

Miranda, running to catch up.

'He can't have,' snapped Holly.

She was annoyed. Partly because their trip to the library had been a failure, and she'd not found out enough about the Kane story even to get started on a decent mystery column for the school newsletter.

But mostly she was annoyed because of what Peter had done. Stealing anything, even the page of an old newspaper, just wasn't right – especially for a Mystery Kid.

Holly rapped firmly on the door. Peter opened it almost at once. He was clearly feeling very pleased with himself.

'I thought it might be you two,' he said. 'Come in, come in. Have I got a surprise for you!'

'Oh, yes?' said Holly, stepping into the hallway.

'Yes siree! Guess what – I've got it!'

'We know,' Miranda said coolly. She wasn't quite so fussed as Holly about the newspaper-ripping. But for Peter to be a jump ahead of them – now, that *was* unforgivable.

Peter frowned. 'You know? How?'

'We don't reveal our methods,' said Miranda. 'Just accept the fact that we know. Everything!'

she added dramatically.

'Yes,' said Holly. 'And we're surprised at you. Aren't we, Miranda?'

'We didn't think you'd go that far, Peter.'

Peter looked at the two girls. 'What do you mean? I did it for the Mystery Kids.'

Holly shook her head. 'Peter, stealing is never right.'

'Stealing?' said Peter, dumbfounded. 'What are you on about, Holly? I earned it. Through sheer hard work. Those newspapers are heavy, you know.'

'Well, one of them isn't quite so heavy now, is it?' said Miranda. 'And we know why, don't we?'

'What?'

'Come on, come on,' said Miranda, closing the door to the flat and waving Peter forward, 'you can show it to us now.'

Shaking his head, Peter led them through the flat and into his small, neat bedroom. Taking a key from his pocket, he started fiddling with the lock on the drawer of his desk.

'Under lock and key, eh?' said Miranda. 'Good thinking, Peter. There are some dishonest people around.'

The drawer slid open. Peter put his hand

in and pulled out a collection of five-pound notes.

It was Holly's turn to look stunned. 'Peter – that's money.'

'Of course it's money,' said Peter. '*My* money. What do you think I've been trying to tell you? I've got it. Enough to buy the surprise I've been talking about!'

'But what about the newspaper?' said Holly.

'Oh, I've still got to deliver *them*. At least until Saturday. But I persuaded Harry at the One-Stop shop to pay me my wages in advance . . .'

'Not *your* newspapers!' exclaimed Miranda. '*The* newspaper! The one in the library.'

'In the library?'

'The one you tore the robbery article out of.'

'Tore? Me? In the library?'

Peter sat down on his bed and looked at them. 'I think you'd better start from the beginning,' he said. 'I haven't been to the library for a week.'

'And you thought I would do a thing like that?' said Peter, after Holly and Miranda had told him about their trip to the library and the discovery of the torn newspaper.

Holly looked at her shoes. 'Sorry, Peter.'

Miranda apologised too. 'It wasn't Holly's fault. She didn't think you would do anything like that. I did.'

'Oh, you did, did you?' said Peter. 'Why? Do I look like a villain?'

'Well, your eyebrows are quite close together,' said Miranda.

Holly couldn't stop herself bursting out laughing. She described the newspaper photograph. Peter laughed too, then.

'He was as shifty looking as they come,' said Miranda. 'And mean with it.' She sucked her teeth. 'Nasty piece of work. That row of stitches . . .'

'Well, at least I haven't got any of them,' said Peter.

'You would have had, if Holly had got hold of you on Saturday morning,' said Miranda. She drew her finger across her throat and let out a blood-curdling groan.

Holly joined in the laughter, happy that they were all back on good terms again. Then she said, 'So if the Newspaper Ripper wasn't you, Peter, and it wasn't us . . . who was it?'

'Mice?' suggested Miranda.

'Miranda,' said Holly, 'be sensible.'

'They do like paper though,' said Peter. 'Harry's had some in the storeroom of the shop. He's going mad. They chewed through some magazines last week before he found out about them.'

'We could go back to the library,' said Holly. 'And ask the librarian for a description of the person who came in before us.'

'Go back and see Vera the Vampire?' Miranda shook her head. 'No way!'

'I'm not sure that would help anyway,' said Peter. 'She wouldn't have known the person's name, would she? And without that, what help would it be?'

'Good thinking, Peter,' said Miranda. 'Forget that idea, Holly.'

Holly sucked the end of her pen. She'd already started a file on the Kane story, sitting up in bed the Friday before to copy out the snippet from the 'Ten years ago today' column. Now she flipped her notebook open and looked at it again.

'Who would want this information – no, who would want the information we *haven't* got?'

'Somebody like us, who saw the article in the paper,' said Peter.

'And is hoping to find the money?' said Holly.

'What we need to work out,' suggested Peter, 'is what that article could have contained.'

'Maybe it would help if we could work out what that headline said,' Miranda suggested.

Holly passed her notes across to Peter. 'Any idea what the rest could say?'

Peter studied the page for a minute. ' "Chase ends in Pol",' he murmured. 'Chase ends in police arrest, I suppose?'

'That's what I thought,' said Holly. 'Which doesn't help.'

'But it doesn't fit the facts,' Miranda pointed out. 'Look. Capital "P". Wouldn't "Chase ends in police arrest" give you a small "p", not a capital? Especially if there's a small "e" in "ends".'

'Miranda could be right, Holly,' said Peter.

'Perhaps we should forget the headline,' said Holly. 'And concentrate on something else.'

'Like what?' said Miranda.

'Like what use that article would have been to somebody wanting to find that missing

40

money.'

Holly racked her brains. What could that article have had in it? What did she put in the articles she wrote? Of course!

'Facts!' she cried.

'What sort of facts? How much money? We know that – fifty thousand pounds.'

Holly read through what she'd written in her notes. 'What don't we know? We know *when* he picked up that money.'

'Five-thirty in the evening,' said Peter. 'Though I don't suppose that's important.'

'What else?'

'We know where he picked it up,' said Miranda. 'Highgate station.'

'But we don't know where Kane was *caught*!' said Holly. 'That's what the newspaper article would have told us!'

'Why is that important?' said Miranda.

'Because by the time he was caught, Kane had got rid of the money.'

'Oh, I get it,' said Miranda. 'If you know where Shifty started and where he ended up . . .'

'You can work out some of the routes he might have taken,' said Holly.

'And where he might have hidden the

money?' Peter shook his head. 'I agree. But the police must have done all that ten years ago. It didn't help them find the money though, did it?'

'No. But for somebody starting from scratch, that article would be pretty helpful. It would give them an idea of where to start looking, wouldn't it?' It was a good enough motive for Holly. She pointed her pencil at the other two. 'I think,' she said, 'someone else is looking for that money.'

'Who?'

'Somebody who saw that piece in Friday's paper. Somebody like . . .' Holly thought hard. 'I don't know,' she said finally.

Peter stood up and waved his money. 'Well, even if somebody else is looking for that money, as of this afternoon *we* are going to have something working for us that nobody else will have.'

'We are?' said Miranda.

Peter took the lead. 'Come on, it's time to go. I can't wait any longer.'

'Go? Go where?'

'You'll see. They were still in the window this morning. I checked as I went by. You're going to love them.'

5 Brainwave

'Phew, that's a relief,' said Peter. 'They're still there.'

They were standing outside a small shop. It was at the top end of a narrow lane that until a few minutes ago Holly hadn't even known existed. One minute Peter had been leading the way down the familiar High Street, the next he had turned sharp left, then left again, to bring them to this point.

'Not many people know about this place,' said Peter, as if he'd been reading her thoughts. 'I only found it by accident. That's probably why nobody's snapped them up before now.' He looked away from the window to Holly and Miranda. 'Well – what do you think?'

Holly didn't know what to think, because she couldn't quite work out what it was that Peter was showing them. He seemed to have brought them to a sort of electronics junk shop. The window was full to bursting with bits of equipment. Things with dials, or switches, or bits of wire – often all three – were everywhere.

'Er . . . good!' said Holly. In the middle of the window she'd spotted a pack of cassette tapes. 'Just the thing. They would save a lot of writing. Good thinking, Peter.'

'What?'

'The cassette tapes. We could record interviews.'

'On the cassette recorder we haven't got,' said Miranda, sniffing and looking up and down the lane. A delicious smell of food was coming from somewhere.

'Not those,' said Peter. He pointed into the window. 'Behind them. See – in the blue box.'

Holly looked again. Tucked away behind the cassette tapes she saw the box Peter meant. It seemed to have been in the window for a while.

'Walkie-talkies? You're going to buy a walkie-talkie set?'

'Two-way radios,' corrected Peter. 'But,

yes. That's it. That's the surprise. Good, eh?'

'Brilliant,' groaned Miranda.

Peter tried to ignore her lack of enthusiasm. 'Just think,' he said, 'we can observe suspicious people from different places, and keep in touch with one another.'

'Or carry out investigations and report back to base,' said Holly, beginning to think about the possibilities.

'We can do that already,' said Miranda. 'From one of those glass thingies you see on street corners. What do they call them now? I remember – telephone boxes!'

'But what if we're not near a telephone box?' said Holly.

'Or our suspect is on the move?' said Peter. 'Walkie-talkies let us keep in touch *and* stay on the move.'

'The police wouldn't have them if they weren't useful, would they?' said Holly. 'I think it's a great idea.'

'And it *is* my money,' said Peter, looking determined. 'I earned it. So I'm going to spend it on what I want.'

He pushed open the shop door, causing a loud buzzer to sound.

'Miranda,' said Holly as she went to follow him in, 'Peter's right. They're just what the Mystery Kids need!'

Miranda bit her lip. Peter, and now Holly, were so keen. How could she say she wasn't? Instead, she peered inside the cramped shop and said, 'Look, there isn't room for three of us in there. I'll see you back here, right?'

'Why?' Holly said. 'Where are you going?'

The delightful smell of baking drifted down the lane again. Miranda sniffed the air. She licked her lips, then rubbed her stomach. Now, there was something she *did* need.

'Guess!'

Miranda drifted back down towards the High Street.

Walkie-talkies! It was all right for Peter and Holly. They liked using cameras and computers and all that technology stuff. So did she, really – it was just that technology didn't seem to like her!

At school, things seemed to have a habit of turning themselves off when she wanted them turned on. Or else, when she was absolutely certain she'd turned off whatever it was they were using, suddenly it would start beeping and flashing at her as if it had a mind of its own.

Walkie-talkies! What was wrong with plain old pencils and paper and using your brains?

Like the mystery of that missing newspaper. They had half a headline, didn't they? OK, so she'd joked a bit about 'Chase ends in Pol', but it should be possible to work out something more from that. And a pair of walkie-talkies wouldn't be any help at all.

She twitched her nose. The smell of doughnuts and cinnamon buns was getting stronger.

Forget it, Miranda, she said to herself. *There's a bakery around here somewhere. If you're a detective of any sort at all you'll be able to find it and be back again in a jiffy.*

Back again. Good point. This little turning behind the High Street was a new one to her, too. Reaching the end of the lane, she looked up at the street sign on the corner so that she knew where to come back to.

Pollards Lane.

Miranda walked on. Then stopped. ' "Chase ends in Pol"?' she said aloud.

She stared up at the street sign. Pollards Lane? Could that headline have said, could it possibly have said, 'Chase ends in Pollards Lane'?

Moments later, she had forgotten all about cinnamon buns and was dashing back towards the electronics shop.

In the shop, the deal had been done. The shopkeeper – a short, wrinkled man with wispy grey hair – had already pulled the blue box from the window. Peter almost snatched it from him.

'They are in good working order, aren't they?'

'Perfect working order,' said the shopkeeper. 'Complete with batteries.'

'Really? That's good.'

'An absolute bargain. One of the best we've ever offered in all my years here. Now, if I can explain how they work . . .'

'I think I know,' said Peter.

'I don't, Peter,' said Holly. 'Not really.'

'There's nothing to it.'

The shopkeeper's face wrinkled a little more as he smiled. 'Perhaps I should explain, then.' He looked up briefly as Miranda charged through the door. 'First, the on/off switch . . .'

As the shopkeeper began his explanation, Holly felt a tug on her sleeve. 'Holly! I think I've got it!'

'Hang on, Miranda.'

'Holl – yyy!'

'Hang *on*, Miranda, please! I want to listen to this. It could be important.'

Miranda stood by impatiently while the shopkeeper rambled on about the on/off switch and how to press the 'talk' button when you wanted to talk and how this made the other handset 'pop' so that you knew when to listen.

'Range and frequency?' Peter asked when the shopkeeper finally stopped talking.

A chuckle. 'Don't worry about the frequency. You won't call the police by accident!'

The shopkeeper carried on, not noticing Peter's slightly disappointed look. 'As to range, well . . . that depends a bit on where you are and what's in between the two handsets. Tall buildings don't help. Oh, and they may get a bit crackly if you're near something electrical like a television, or something metal like a radiator.'

'So don't use them while you're sitting on

the radiator watching television, Peter,' joked Miranda. She grabbed Holly by the elbow and led her away. '*Now* can I say something?'

'Yes.' Holly looked over to where the wrinkled shopkeeper was still talking to Peter. 'He does go on a bit, doesn't he?'

Miranda came straight to the point. 'Pollards Lane.'

'Sorry?'

'Pollards Lane. This is Pollards Lane. I didn't know there was a Pollards Lane round here.'

'Neither did I,' said Holly. She shrugged. 'So?'

Miranda stood on tiptoe to look straight into Holly's eyes. '*Pollards* Lane. *Pol*-lards Lane. Holly, what if the "Pol" in that headline wasn't the first part of "police" but the first part of . . .'

'Pollards?' said Holly. 'You mean what if it said something like, "Chase ends in Pollards Lane"?'

'Right!'

'Here? In this lane?'

Miranda looked out to the shop's front. Apart from a man wearing a bobble hat walking hurriedly past with a clipboard in his hand, the lane was deathly quiet. 'OK, so it doesn't look like anything's ever happened here. But it *might* have, mightn't it?'

Holly nodded thoughtfully. 'How could we find out?'

'Well,' said Miranda. She nodded towards the shopkeeper. 'We could ask Mr Chatterbox, there. Maybe he was working here then.'

Holly gazed round the shop. Judging from the collection in the window, it certainly looked as though it had been in business for a fair while. And the shopkeeper *had* said that Peter's bargain was one of the best that had been offered in all his years here.

'OK,' she whispered. 'But how?'

'Follow me,' said Miranda. She strode down to the cash desk, talking as she went.

'You know, Holly, I read in the paper the other day about that thing they do in Spain where they let all the bulls out of their pens for the afternoon and let them chase people up and down lanes just like this one.'

The shopkeeper looked up from wrapping the walkie-talkie set. 'Ever get any bulls charging down here?' Miranda asked.

The shopkeeper smiled quietly and shook his head. 'No, nothing too noisy. Usually.'

Holly caught on to the idea. 'How about police chases? Didn't I read somewhere about a chase that ended in Pollards Lane?'

The shopkeeper shook his head again. 'No. Not – well – unless you mean the Kane chase. But that was years ago.'

'Kane?' said Holly. Had they hit the jackpot?

'I think that was his name,' said the shopkeeper, rubbing his chin. 'It was certainly something like that. Dear me, though. What excitement! Oh, I remember it as though it was yesterday. It took me quite some time to get over it, I can tell you.'

'Why, what happened?' asked Miranda. She gave Holly and Peter a look of triumph.

'It was about six o'clock. I'd just closed the shop and was washing out my sandwich box – I'd had salad cream that day, and it had gone everywhere – anyway, then I heard all this shouting going on, so I rushed out to see what was happening.'

'And what *was* happening?' said Holly, wondering if they would ever find out.

'Well, apparently a policeman – don't ask me his name, I'm hopeless at remembering names —'

'Jenkins,' said Holly. 'PC Alan Jenkins.'

'Really? Anyway, this policeman had spotted this chap Kane walking as calm as you like down the High Street. Kane had seen him just in time and dashed off, but he couldn't have known much about the area, because he ran down Pollards Lane, and Pollards Lane goes nowhere . . . well, except to the garages at the back. Anyway, I came out just as the policeman rugby-tackled him. Right outside here! *Right outside!* I saw everything!'

'Any blood?' asked Miranda.

'Miranda,' said Peter. 'You ghoul!'

'Stitches, remember?' said Miranda. 'Above the cheekbone.'

'Blood, you say?' The shopkeeper nodded. 'Funny you should mention that. One of them did have some blood on his face. Which one was it now . . . ?'

'Kane,' said Miranda. 'It must have been Kane.'

'Must it? Anyway . . . the policeman must have called for help – he had a two-way radio just like you've got there, young man,' the shopkeeper said. 'And that was it. Yes, I remember it as if it was yesterday.'

'Kane wasn't carrying a case? You didn't see any money?'

'Money? No, no. That was the big mystery apparently. He'd collected a case stuffed with money. But by the time he got here, he'd dumped it. He wouldn't say where. Even at the trial, if I remember right. That's probably why the judge gave him such a long sentence.'

'Long? How long?' asked Holly.

The shopkeeper shook his head. 'Oh, I can't remember exactly. I remember thinking, "Hmm, that's a long sentence" when I heard about it though.'

'No idea at all?' Holly persisted.

The shopkeeper rubbed his chin. 'Double figures, I'm pretty sure of that. Yes, I remember now. "At least ten years", that's what the judge said he should serve.'

'Ten years?'

A sudden thought struck Holly. All this happened ten years ago . . . and Ginger Kane was sentenced to ten years in jail.

'So,' she said, 'he could be getting out of jail round about now?'

The shopkeeper gave this some thought. 'Hmm. When you put it like that . . . yes. Yes, I suppose he could.'

6 Are you receiving?

'MK-one to MK-two. Are you receiving, MK-two? Over.'

Holly pushed in the talk button on the handset she was holding and held it to her mouth.

'MK-two here. Receiving you loud and clear, MK-one. Over.' She turned to Miranda. 'These are *brilliant*!'

Holly held down the talk button again. 'MK-two to MK-one. Can you see anything suspicious?'

Peter's voice crackled back. 'Nothing as yet, MK-two. Can you?'

Miranda leaned over Holly's shoulder. 'Only you, over on the other side of the road, looking as though you're talking to yourself!'

They stopped by a lamppost and looked across the road. A bus came along and stopped to pick up passengers, blocking their view. When it moved off they saw Peter. He'd stopped and was looking across at them. Moments later his voice came through again.

'This is only a test, MK-two. Only a test.'

'The name's Miranda,' said Miranda in a voice that Holly thought might almost be loud enough for Peter to hear without walkie-talkies. 'Miranda. Not MK-two, whatever that's supposed to mean!'

'I explained all that yesterday,' said Peter. 'It's your call sign.'

'MK for Mystery Kids,' said Holly.

'Yes, yes, I heard all that.'

'So when I put out a call to MK-two, you know I'm trying to contact you.'

'Who else is there, then?'

'Nobody, of course.' Peter's crackling voice sounded impatient. 'But that's not the point. It's just the way you do it. The actual call sign isn't important.'

'Then why are you MK-one, and us MK-two? Why can't we be MK-one?'

Peter lost patience. 'How about you being MK-zero, Miranda?'

Miranda put her hands on her hips and

yelled across the road. 'Just watch it, Peter Hamilton! Just watch it!'

Holly took her finger off the talk button so that Peter couldn't hear what she said. 'They're his walkie-talkies, Miranda,' she said. 'So if he wants to be MK-one, he can be MK-one. It doesn't matter, does it?'

'No,' sighed Miranda. 'I suppose not.'

Holly held out the handset. 'Come on. It's your turn.'

Miranda shook her head. 'No, it's all right. You can have my turn.'

Holly didn't need any persuading. Walkie-talkies! Just what *real* undercover teams used! She really felt as though the Mystery Kids were doing things properly now, whispering secret orders and codes that would travel unseen through the air. Even Harriet the Spy would be impressed! Harriet was Holly and Miranda's heroine, even though she only existed in a book.

She pressed the talk button again. 'MK-one?' Holly said into the handset, trying to make her voice crisp and authoritative. 'MK-two calling. Suspicious character spotted. We are following. Repeat, we are following. Keep this line open.'

She veered away across the pavement. Miranda broke into a trot to catch her up. 'What are you on about?'

'It's a test.' She pointed ahead, to where a stout lady with two carrier bags was shoving her way towards a small group of market stalls. 'We're following her.'

Holly spoke into the handset again. 'MK-one, our suspect is wearing a long brown coat and carrying two shopping bags. We are in visual contact. Stand by for further orders.'

'Further orders?' laughed Miranda. 'Peter won't like the sound of *that*!'

But Holly was already ducking between two stalls as the woman put a spurt on.

'It's not a case of orders,' said Holly. 'We're working as a team. This is known as zone surveillance.'

'Zone *what*?'

'Look. Imagine that lady is a secret agent.'

'From the size of her she's more likely to be a double agent,' said Miranda. 'But go on.'

'If one of us follows her everywhere she could get suspicious. But with Peter's walkie-talkies we can share the job. Our zone is on this side of the road, Peter's is on the other side. We watch her here, then when she crosses over, Peter watches her.'

'What if she gets knocked down by a bus halfway across?'

'Then we all watch her! Oh, Miranda! I thought you would be as keen as me about these walkie-talkies.'

'And *I* thought we were going to Highgate station. Remember? We wanted to see where Ginger Kane picked up that case full of money, so that *you* could describe where the chase began in the mystery column.'

'We *are* going to the station,' said Holly. She ducked down the side of a clothes stall as the stout woman turned and looked in their direction. 'But this is *fun*. Come on Miranda, this isn't like you.'

'Right, Holly Adams,' said Miranda, deciding it was time to throw herself into this game. 'You asked for it. Report this lot back to MK-one.'

She ducked down into the middle of a carousel of woolly jumpers, then popped her head out. 'Suspect is feeling produce on fruit stall,' she whispered dramatically. 'Maybe her contact has left something there for her. Maybe it's a plant. No it's not, it's a tomato. She's planting a tomato-shaped bomb! Tell MK-one to clear his side of the street. Emergency! Emergency!'

She swung the carousel round, causing a bobble-hatted man with a clipboard to dodge hurriedly to one side.

'Watch it, stupid!' the man growled as he went by.

'Miranda,' whispered Holly. 'Stop messing about. You nearly ran him over!'

Next to her, Miranda shouted again.

She'd changed roles. Now she was a submarine commander.

'Up periscope,' she cried, bobbing her head above the carousel and swinging round in an arc. 'Battleship on the starboard bow. Tell MK-one to prepare torpedoes!'

She ducked down, then bobbed up again. As she shouted, 'Battleship ahoy! Fire one!' the stout woman with the carrier bags looked their way.

'Fire two!' yelled Miranda, just as the woman finished buying what she wanted and turned away from the stall. 'Come on Holly, what's MK-one doing? Fire two! Holly! Holly! Are you playing this game or not?'

Next to her, Holly seemed to be staring at something.

'Miranda,' she whispered. 'It's him!'

'What?'

'Him! Look!' She pointed beyond the fruit stall.

'There. The man in the grey raincoat. It's him. The face in the paper. The blackmailer. Ginger Kane!'

Miranda stood up in the middle of the carousel. 'Where?'

'There!' pointed Holly. The man was on the move now, weaving between shoppers as he moved towards the main road.

'I don't know,' said Miranda. She formed a pair of pretend binoculars out of her hands and looked through them. As the man briefly turned their way, she put them down again. 'But it could be. It *definitely* could be. He looks older than the man in the picture, though.'

'Well, he would after ten years in jail, wouldn't he?' said Holly. 'You look older than you were ten years ago, don't you?'

'I should hope so,' snorted Miranda. 'Ten years ago I was still in a pushchair.'

The man was almost out of the market area now. Desperately, Holly fumbled for the walkie-talkie handset and pressed the talk button.

'Peter! Peter, are you there?'

'MK-one here. You forgot to use your call-sign, MK-two.'

'Peter, we haven't got time for all that. Listen, this is for real. Kane – the one whose picture was in the newspaper. He must be out of jail. We've just seen him!'

'Where?'

'In the market. He's just leaving, Peter. He's coming your way. Can you see him?'

Peter answered. 'What does he look like? I didn't see the picture, remember.'

'Grey raincoat. Dark hair, thin on top. Can you see him, Peter?'

'No.'

'Then where — '

'Yes! Yes, I see him. You're sure it's him?'

'Definitely.'

'Right. I'm on his tail, MK-two.'

Holly and Miranda looked at each other. Miranda smiled sheepishly. 'OK. So walkie-talkies might have their uses. Let's go!'

Ducking down again, she shoved her way out through the woolly jumpers – and straight into the stallholder.

'Are you buying *one* of them?' he growled, 'or *all* of them?'

Miranda was just about to mutter something about leaving her purse at home when another voice broke into the conversation.

It was the voice of the stout woman with the brown coat. She was holding two carrier bags.

'Oi! Who've you been calling a battleship?'

'I thought we'd *never* get away!' said Holly as they finally convinced the stout lady they hadn't been talking about her. They ran out to the main road.

Miranda looked up and down. 'No sign of him. Or Peter.'

Holly pulled out the walkie-talkie handset and switched it on. Immediately it crackled into life. 'Holly, where have you been?'

'We got sort of held up. I switched off. What's happening, Peter?'

Peter's voice came through. It sounded a little faint. 'I'm following him. He seems to be dodging about a bit.'

Holly pressed the talk button. 'How do you mean?'

'Going into shop doorways. Pretending to look at things in the window.'

'How does he know he's pretending?' asked Miranda. Holly repeated the question.

'Because he doesn't stay long enough to be really looking,' replied Peter. 'He keeps leaning out. Then he checks both ways before moving on. He's doing it now.'

Peter's voice faded for a moment, then came back again. 'He's on the move again.'

'Peter,' said Holly, 'where are you?'

The handset she was holding made a faint sound. She held it closer to her ear. Peter's voice seemed really far away now. 'Peter!' she shouted, holding the talk button down. 'Speak up. I can't hear you!'

She got no answer.

7 Spot-the-crook

'Flat batteries!' spluttered Jamie. Holly's obnoxious little brother dived behind a chair as she threw a pencil at him.

Out of view, and out of range, he settled down to a game of pretend cosmic soldiers, complete with sound effects.

'It could have happened to anyone,' muttered Peter, looking very sheepish. 'They must have run down while the set was in the shop window.'

Holly made a quick note in the section of her notebook headed General Spying Equipment. 'Remember to carry spare batteries *everywhere*.'

They were settled in armchairs in the sitting-room at Holly's house. Mrs Adams had just come home from work and was busy making something that smelt good in the kitchen. Miranda and Peter had been invited to stay for tea.

'So, what happened after we lost contact with you?' said Holly. She didn't notice that, behind the chair, everything had gone quiet.

'Well,' said Peter, happy for a chance to change the subject, 'I followed him up the High Street. Then he turned right.'

'He didn't see you?'

'No. There was a fair number of people going the same way. They all seemed to be in a hurry.'

Holly looked up from her note-taking. 'He was going to Highgate station, wasn't he?'

Peter looked impressed. 'How did you know?'

'I looked at my watch when the walkie-talkies went dead. It was just about half-past four. The rush hour was just starting.'

'Conclusion – lots of people hurrying towards the tube station on their way home from work,' said Miranda. 'Well done, Holly.'

'Well, as it happens you're right,' said Peter. 'That's where he was going.'

The very place where Kane had collected the money ten years earlier! Holly wrote 'Highgate station' in her notebook and underlined it.

'What happened when he got to the station, Peter?'

'He bought a newspaper and leaned against the wall for a couple of minutes. But it didn't look to me as though he was reading it.'

'Why?'

'He didn't turn the page over once.'

'Maybe he's a slow reader?' suggested Miranda.

'He seemed to be looking over the top of it.'

'Checking that he hadn't been followed?' Holly wondered aloud.

Peter shrugged. 'Then he got his ticket out of his pocket, put it into the automatic barrier and went through.'

'You didn't buy a ticket and follow him, then?'

'I couldn't,' said Peter.

'Why not?'

'By then it was gone half-past four. I was late for my round. Harry's One-Stop isn't that far from the station, so I went straight there.'

'Now then,' said Holly. 'We need to work out what's going on here. Let's go through the facts as we know them.'

She started writing. 'One – ten years ago, a case containing fifty thousand pounds went missing somewhere between Highgate station and Pollards Lane.'

'Two,' said Miranda, 'a couple of days ago a newspaper article about what happened that day was torn out of the library's copy of the *Highgate Herald*.'

'And three,' said Peter, 'you think the man who was pictured in that article . . .'

'Ginger Kane, otherwise known as Shifty,' added Miranda.

'. . . is out of jail and back in Highgate,' continued Peter. 'Don't you think that's a bit of a coincidence?'

Holly nodded thoughtfully. 'It could be. But you heard what Mr Chatterbox at the electronics shop said – Kane was sent to prison for ten years.'

'At least,' said Miranda.

'So, he *could* just have got out.'

'And *could* just have come back to recover the money,' said Miranda.

Holly's eyes lit up. 'Which might explain the torn newspaper. It could have been him who got there before us!'

Peter shook his head. 'That doesn't make sense, Holly. Why would Ginger Kane want to take that piece out of the newspaper? He *knows* where he went that day.'

'But remember what Mr Chatterbox said? Kane couldn't have known much about the area because he ran down Pollards Lane, and Pollards Lane doesn't go anywhere. Maybe he *doesn't* know where he went that day. Maybe he needed the newspaper cutting to find out!'

'And he *was* acting suspiciously when you followed him, wasn't he, Peter?' said Miranda.

'Ye-es,' Peter said uncertainly. 'He did *seem* to be looking out for something . . .'

'Like what's happened to the place where he hid the money!' exclaimed Holly. 'Now *that* would make sense, wouldn't it?'

'Possibly,' said Peter, 'but I'd have said he was acting more like a man looking out for somebody.'

'Makes sense,' said a voice from behind a chair.

As the three of them turned towards the sudden sound, Jamie popped his head out from his hiding-place. They'd completely forgotten about him.

'If he's just been let out, then the police will know, won't they? *And* they'll know that if he wants that money he's got to come and get it, so they'll be looking out for him just in case he does.'

'Jamie,' Holly said automatically, 'you don't know what you're talking about.'

'I do, too,' said Jamie, diving back behind the chair.

'Hang on, Holly,' whispered Miranda. 'Think about it. If the police do know Kane's been let out, then *he'll* know that *they* know, won't he?'

Holly thought about it. 'So,' she said slowly, 'if he has come back then *he'll* be looking out for *them*, too.'

Before they had a chance to discuss this new idea further, Mrs Adams called them to the table.

To Holly's surprise, Mr Adams came through the front door at just that moment.

'Ta-raa!' he proclaimed. 'Diaries and red pens out. Kindly record the fact that today I was home in time for tea.'

'Oh,' said Jamie. 'Does that mean there'll be less for me?'

'I do hope so, Jamie,' said Mr Adams, loosening his tie and sitting down at the table. 'Solicitors need to eat too, you know.'

Mrs Adams sat next to him, with Jamie

opposite. Holly, Peter and Miranda sat together at the end of the table. It wasn't until they were well into their second piece of chicken that Holly thought again about what Jamie had said.

'Do you suppose Jamie could be right?' she whispered to Miranda.

'What, about Ginger Kane looking out for the police? I suppose so.'

'It *is* logical,' whispered Peter. 'He would be worried.'

Holly looked at Jamie and shook her head. 'But he's never been right about *anything*.'

'Oh, yes I have!' said Jamie, gulping down a chip so quickly that he broke out in a fit of coughing. Mrs Adams had to rush to the rescue with a glass of water.

'Yes, you have been what?' she said.

'Right,' said Jamie, wiping his eyes. 'About lots of things.'

Mrs Adams looked straight at Holly. 'I know I may regret this but what is Jamie talking about?'

Holly shrugged. 'Has he been out in the sun?'

'They think they've seen a man whose picture was in the paper for doing a robbery

71

years and years ago,' said Jamie with a smirk. 'Ginger Coin or something.'

'Ginger Kane,' said Holly.

'They think he's come back to pick up his loot.'

Mr Adams looked up from his newspaper. 'Holly,' he said in a tone that Holly knew meant business, 'what is going on?'

'We were just testing my new walkie-talkies, Mr Adams,' said Peter.

'And we saw a man. He looked like somebody we'd seen in the paper recently.'

'Ginger Kane? I believe he was released recently. But . . .' Mr Adams sighed patiently. 'What did this man look like?'

'Shifty,' Miranda put in at once. 'Dead shifty.'

'Inadmissible as evidence,' said Mr Adams. 'Conjecture, not fact. Any real detail?'

'Thin on top,' said Peter.

'*Very*,' said Miranda. 'Almost as thin on top as my father.'

'I'm sure he'll thank you for that, Miranda.'

Miranda went pink for the first time Holly could remember. 'Case dismissed,' said Mr Adams.

'Why?' said Holly.

'If that was the man you saw, then it couldn't have been Ginger Kane. How do you think Ginger Kane got his nickname?'

'Not – his hair?' gulped Holly.

'Thick and curly,' said Mr Adams. 'Even after a hundred years in jail, Ginger Kane wouldn't be thin on top.'

'OK,' said Peter, 'so you got it wrong.'

'I suppose so,' said Holly. 'But I was so *certain*.'

'It was a good test of the walkie-talkies, though,' said Peter, trying to look on the bright side.

'It certainly was,' said Miranda.

Peter looked at her in surprise. 'You really think so?'

'Oh, yes. Now you know *exactly* how long the batteries last!'

'Oh, let's not argue,' said Holly.

They sat in silence for a while. They were in Holly's room, the one Jamie-free place in the house.

'Still,' Peter said finally. 'It's a good piece for your mystery column all the same. And I think Holly's idea for the competition is great.'

'Really?' said Holly.

'Yes, really,' said Peter.

Holly brightened. Peter was right. They *could* still use the story. Sitting on her bed, Holly tucked her knees beneath her chin as she thought. 'We could draw a map of the area,' she said, 'and write what we know of what happened.'

'That it started at Highgate station, and ended in Pollards Lane.'

'They could be marked on the map.'

'And that it was all over in twenty-five minutes,' said Miranda. She had moved Holly's bean-bag into the centre of the floor and was curled up in it like a hamster.

' "Use your skill and judgement to decide where the money was hidden. Put your 'X' on the map." '

'Just like those spot-the-ball competitions,' Holly said. 'The winner will be the person who, in the opinion of the judges . . .'

'. . . puts their cross on the exact centre of the loot,' laughed Miranda.

'Well, where the judges think the loot is,' said Holly.

'And who are the judges going to be?' asked Peter.

Holly and Miranda looked at each other, nodded, then looked at Peter. 'Us, of course,' they said together.

'So how are the judges going to decide where the loot is?'

'Er . . . good question.' What Holly liked about Peter was the way he could see what questions needed to be answered. What she *didn't* like about him was the way he asked them!

'We'll have to work it out for ourselves. Is that what you're saying?'

'I'd say you've got to come up with an answer of *some* sort,' said Peter. 'One you can justify. I don't see how you can pick a winner otherwise. To do this properly you're going to have to think like a criminal.'

'No problem,' said Miranda.

'Put ourselves in Kane's position, you mean?' said Holly. 'Imagine that we've just picked up that money?'

Peter nodded. 'Yes. What would you do?'

'Run for it,' said Miranda at once. 'Until I dropped.'

'*I* wouldn't,' said Holly. 'I'd walk. Running would attract too much attention. I'd walk normally.'

'Not with a big beefy rugby-tackling police-man after you, you wouldn't,' said Miranda.

'He wasn't after him at first.'

'Kane didn't know that.'

'All right,' said Holly. 'So I would run until I thought I was safe. *Then* I would walk.'

'With fifty thousand pounds on you?'

Holly lay back on her bed and studied the ceiling. It wasn't easy thinking like a criminal. She knew how she'd felt trying to get out of the library when they hadn't done anything wrong at all! Then something occurred to her. 'He didn't have the money on him all the time, did he?'

'Right,' said Miranda. 'He must have spent some time hiding it. If he was caught after twenty-five minutes, he probably only ran for – how long? Ten minutes? How far can anyone run in ten minutes?'

'Five thousand metres? Maybe more?' suggested Peter. 'That's what they do at the Olympics.'

Miranda snorted. 'Not carrying cases stuffed with money, they don't!'

Holly leaped from her bed and looked at her bookshelf. She pulled out an old *A–Z* of London and found the page which showed the Highgate area. 'How far is it from Highgate station to Pollards Lane?' she said.

Peter took a ruler from Holly's desk and held it to the page. 'Seven centimetres. At a scale of four-and-a-half centimetres to the kilometre that's what?'

Miranda rolled on to the floor and pulled the bean-bag over her head. 'Leave me out when it comes to mental arithmetic.'

'About one-and-a-half kilometres,' said Peter. 'That's assuming he went by the shortest route. Which is due south . . .' He checked the map again – and gave a little gasp of surprise. 'Hey!'

'Hey what?' said Miranda, popping her head out briefly from under the bean-bag, then popping it back again.

'It would have taken him straight past Harry's One-Stop.'

'If it had been there at the time,' said a muffled Miranda. 'Which it wasn't. Becky and Rachel never stop telling me that they had to wheel me for miles in my push-chair to buy me an ice-cream – as if *they* didn't have one, of course!'

Holly smiled. Her brother Jamie was a big enough pain, but at least he was younger than her. She often pitied Miranda in that way. Having twin *older* sisters to boss you about – like she had – must be awful.

'Still, it's a good road to use for the competition solution isn't it?' she said.

A hand stretched out from beneath the bean-bag and stuck up a thumb.

'Good,' said Holly. 'Now all we have to do is decide how far from the station Ginger Kane would have got. Any ideas?'

The bean-bag shook from side to side.

'I have,' said Peter. 'Try it for yourself.'

8 On the trail

'Right,' said Holly. 'Synchronise watches.'

She and Miranda placed their wrists together. 'We are standing outside Highgate station. And it's now . . . ten-thirty-five precisely. Agreed?'

Miranda nodded. 'The things I do for your mystery column,' she said. 'I'll expect you to come up with some good jokes for me next time.'

'You couldn't use *good* jokes,' Holly said with a grin. 'Anyway, you've got the easy bit. You're only walking. I'm the one doing the running.'

'*And* I've got to ride to Pollards Lane, remember,' said Miranda, patting the saddle of her bike. 'Let's hope I don't run into Mr Chatterbox. I'll never get away!'

'If you don't stop nattering you won't even get there,' said Holly. 'Now, are we clear?'

Miranda nodded. 'As crystal. I'm going to ride to Pollards Lane.'

'Where Ginger Kane was arrested.'

'The very spot. Then, at eleven o'clock precisely, I'm going to start walking your way.'

'Make sure you do, Miranda. Any riding at all and the test won't be right. And you can remember the route we agreed?'

'Of course I can remember.' She frowned. 'What I can't remember is *why* I'm doing it.'

'Because we know Kane had twenty-five minutes.'

'Right . . .'

'And we're assuming he ran for a while, then hid the money, then walked for a while.'

'Ending up near Pollards Lane.'

'Right. Only we don't know how long he was running, or how long he was walking. We only know that he did it all, and hid the money, in twenty-five minutes.'

'So . . .' Miranda said slowly.

'So, for the purposes of the competition, you're going to do what Kane did, only in reverse.'

'Walk due north from Pollards Lane,' said Miranda.

'While, at the same time, I'm going to start from here and run due south towards you.'

'And where we meet,' cried Miranda, 'is the answer to the mystery column competition! Got it!'

'The winner will be the one who puts their "X" closest to that spot,' said Holly. 'At least we'll be able to say the solution fits the facts of the case.' She looked at her watch. 'Come on then, time you were off.'

Miranda hopped on to her bike. 'I notice Peter found a good excuse to get out of this one.'

Holly laughed. 'Helping Harry set mousetraps in the storeroom of the One-Stop? You have to admit, it's original. Anyway, we'll probably see him. Harry's One-Stop is on our route.'

'I thought he'd earned all the money he needed from his paper round.'

'He forgot about the extra batteries,' said Holly. 'This little job will pay for them. Then we'll be able to use the walkie-talkies again.'

'Really?' Miranda's face fell. 'Holly, do we *have* to use those things?'

'Miranda, of course we do. I can't understand why you don't like them. They work brilliantly.'

'For you, maybe,' said Miranda. 'Not for me.'

Holly laughed as Miranda pedalled off. Just under ten minutes, and it would be eleven o'clock.

She paced up and down outside the station for a while, studying the paving stones beneath her feet. To think Ginger Kane himself had stood on this very spot. It gave her a creepy feeling.

She was pleased with the solution they'd come up with, though. It would make for a really interesting mystery column. And if anybody argued with the answer, she'd be able to say they'd actually tried it.

Holly waited as her watch ticked round. Then, as it flicked over to eleven o'clock exactly, she set off.

Two hundred metres along Archway Road was the first turning they'd decided she would take. It was on the right, heading due south, called Highgate Avenue.

'Ginger Kane would have scooted down a side road as quickly as he could,' Miranda had said when they'd studied the map, and Holly had agreed.

Holly ran down it as fast as she could. In her mind she was trying to imagine that she was being chased by a pack of wolves – which is how she thought Ginger Kane must have felt when he knew he was being chased by the police.

It was this that caused her to miss the next turning. 'Left at Southwood Avenue,' they'd agreed. But Holly was so busy imagining that, instead of going left, she went straight on. Before she knew it, the road had veered sharp right, then right again. She ran on – and found herself at the other end of Southwood Avenue! She'd gone round in a circle!

Annoyed at herself for being so stupid, Holly ran on. She checked her watch. The mistake must have cost her at least two minutes. On she went, back to Archway Road for a short distance, then right into Park Road.

She was back on the route they'd agreed, but as to where she'd meet Miranda now . . . the calculations would be all wrong, surely.

Holly ran on. She'd been going for five minutes now, and was starting to feel tired.

Had Ginger Kane felt the same way? Was it at this point he first thought of hiding the money? She looked at the houses as she went by. They were quite old, all with neat gardens. There couldn't have been a hiding- place anywhere here.

Holly sped on, past one turning after another. Park Road was long, with lots of them. At each, Holly looked quickly for any spot that Ginger Kane himself might have noticed. She saw one boarded-up house. But would that have been empty ten years ago?

Holly was panting hard now. Seven minutes were gone. She was going to have to stop soon anyway, before she collapsed. Up ahead, she saw that Park Road was beginning to swing round to the right. Holly remembered the point from the *A–Z* map. It wasn't too far from here to the High Street.

Where *was* Miranda?

Puffing like a steam train, Holly went past a final turning. Her heart was thumping and her eyes were watering with the effort.

Suddenly, everything seemed to happen at once.

As the road turned to the right, Miranda

almost bumped into her as she came the other way.

And, seconds later, the third member of the Mystery Kids shot out of the alleyway.

'There you are,' whispered Peter. 'At last! Come on!'

Holly didn't even have time to catch her breath before Peter added, 'He's here! The man you saw in the photograph!'

They followed Peter down the alleyway, to a pile of cardboard boxes stacked at the end.

'I saw him when I was in the shop,' said Peter, ducking down behind one of the boxes.

Holly crouched beside him. 'Shop? Where are we, Peter?'

Peter looked at her as though she was mad. 'Where?' He patted the brick wall beside him. '*This* is Harry's One-Stop.' He pointed out towards the roadway. 'And *that*'s Lake Road. It's only short, and runs parallel to Park Road.'

'So this alleyway joins the two together?'

'If you like, yes,' said Peter. 'It runs round behind all the back gardens as well.'

'So where is he?' It was Miranda, crawling

past them on her hands and knees to the very end of the alleyway.

'In that car across the road,' whispered Peter. 'I'd just finished helping Harry set the mouse-traps. I saw him when I came out of the storeroom. He's been there for ages. Just sitting, and making notes.'

'Looks like him,' said Miranda, thoughtfully. 'Shifty.' She looked over her shoulder at Peter. 'What do you think he's making notes about?'

'Which times are quiet, and which aren't. If he stashed the money round here somewhere, he'll be wanting to come back when it's quiet, won't he?'

'But . . .' began Holly. She popped her head above the boxes, then popped it back quickly as a man wearing a bobble hat and carrying a clipboard came out of Harry's One-Stop.

'But what?' said Peter.

'But I thought,' said Holly, as she heard the man with the clipboard walk slowly past the end of the alleyway and off down the road, 'we'd agreed he *couldn't* be Ginger Kane.'

Peering over, round and between the cardboard boxes, they studied the man in the car.

'I mean,' Holly said, 'look at him. His hair's not exactly ginger-coloured.'

'More like black,' said Miranda.

'Disguise,' said Peter. 'It could be a disguise.'

'I suppose so . . .' said Holly. 'Watch out!'

They ducked back in again as, across the road, the car door swung open.

'He may have seen us,' hissed Peter. 'Get ready to run!'

'*You* get ready to run,' said Miranda. 'I'm not going anywhere.'

Behind her cardboard box, Holly watched intently as the man got out. Looking both ways, he strolled across the road. He was coming towards them!

He stepped on to the pavement. He walked to the very edge of the alleyway. He was so close that Holly could almost reach out and touch him. But he hadn't seen them – he was looking away down the road. Heart thumping, she looked up at the side of his face as he moved away. Moments later, the door to Harry's One-Stop clicked open.

Miranda whistled under her breath. 'That was close!'

'But did you see it?' whispered Holly.

'See what?' said Peter.

'The scar above his cheekbone! In the photograph he had a row of stitches in just that spot. It *is* him!'

Peter looked at the two girls. 'So – what do we do now?'

Nobody said a thing for a few moments. Then Miranda got to her feet and picked up her bike.

'How about if I just happen to walk up and pretend to have a look in that shop window?'

'Good idea,' said Peter. 'Harry displays advertising cards in his window. You can look at those.'

Miranda edged out of the alleyway. Whistling tunelessly, she wheeled her bike along the pavement. Then, with a loud cry of, 'Oh, I wonder if my runaway tortoise has been found!' she stopped and pretended to examine the advertisements in the shop window.

Suddenly, she seemed to forget everything and shot back into the alleyway again.

'He's in there!'

'We know that.'

'What I mean is,' gasped Miranda, 'he's in

there *talking*. He was waving a card under Harry's nose and *talking* to him.'

'So – why didn't you stay there?'

'Because I've just had this brilliant idea,' said Miranda. 'Peter, you could go in there with one of the walkie-talkies. You get close to Shifty and press your talk button or whatever you do, and bingo – we can all hear what's being said!'

Peter winced. 'I can't do that.'

'Why not?' said Miranda.

Holly nodded. 'It sounds a good idea to me, Peter.'

Peter looked unhappy. 'Because – I haven't got any new batteries yet.'

'Oh, brilliant!' whispered Miranda.

'I was about to buy them,' said Peter. 'But Harry was having a discussion with that man with a clipboard who came out a while ago. Then, as I was waiting, I saw Ginger Kane outside. So I shot out and hid in this alley. I thought it was better to watch him instead.'

Holly nodded. 'Right, Miranda?'

'I suppose so,' Miranda said grudgingly. 'Go on then, Holly, you go and see what's happening.'

But no sooner had Holly reached the end of the alleyway than she was diving back again.

'He's coming out!'

Moments later, Harry's shop door clicked and the man with the scar walked past. He didn't give them a second glance, just looked hard down the road, then ran across to his car. This time he didn't stay around. He started it up and sped off down the road.

'Well, we can't follow him this time, can we?' said Holly.

'Not unless Miranda wants to pedal after him,' said Peter.

'Not today, thank you.'

'But maybe we can find out what he said to Harry,' said Holly thoughtfully. She eased her way out from behind the stack of boxes. 'Come on, Peter. Let's get your batteries.'

As they pushed through the shop door, Holly still wasn't clear exactly how they could ask Harry what had been said. But she was determined to try if the chance arose.

'Hello, Harry,' said Peter. 'I need four batteries, please. This size.' He held up one of the flat batteries.

'As many as that?' said Miranda. 'I hope they last longer than the other ones. Otherwise your paper-round money won't be lasting long, either.'

The shopkeeper took a pack of four of the correct size batteries from the shelf behind him. As he heard Miranda, he said, 'That reminds me, Peter. Can you get in earlier than usual tomorrow afternoon? I've got a bit of a . . . problem.'

He looked flustered, Holly thought. She nudged Peter in the ribs.

'A problem, Harry?' said Peter. 'Anything I can do to help?'

Harry shook his head. 'No. I just need to get the deliveries over and done with nice and early. That's all.'

Flustered, thought Holly. *He's definitely flustered*. It had to be something to do with what Ginger Kane had said. What was it? And why should he want Peter there early?

'Early closing day, is it?' asked Holly innocently.

As Harry fumbled with Peter's change, Holly sensed she'd said the right thing. Moments later she was certain of it.

'A man . . . er . . . from the council. Just been here,' stammered Harry. 'Told me he needs to close the shop for the weekend.'

Holly and Miranda pricked up their ears as Peter echoed, 'From the council?'

'That's what his card said,' said Harry. 'Needs to look everywhere, he says. In the storeroom, everywhere. See if I need any work done.'

'Work?' said Holly. 'What sort of work?'

'Oh, I don't know,' grumbled Harry. 'Treatment,' he said. 'For dry rot. The houses round here have got it, so he says. And as the shop was built on the foundations of one of them he reckons this place needs to be checked too.'

Still grumbling, Harry put the batteries in a small paper bag and Peter's money in the till. 'Dry rot!' he said. 'I ask you. The shop was only built ten years ago.'

Alarm bells started jangling in Holly's head. 'Ten years?' she said, trying not to look excited. 'Only as long as that?'

Harry nodded. He seemed to be feeling easier. 'I spotted the need, see,' he said proudly. 'A lot of people were moving into this area and there wasn't a general store for them. There was an abandoned house here, so I sank my savings into having it knocked down and this shop built on top of it.'

'Ten years ago?' said Holly again. 'You mean this shop was actually being *built* ten years ago?'

'As near as makes no difference,' said Harry. 'What's the date today?'

'August 26th,' Holly said quickly.

'Well, I opened on the 30th of September. At this time ten years ago – oh, they would have been laying the floorboards.'

'It all fits together!' cried Holly. 'This time it really *does* fit together!'

'It certainly looks like it,' said Peter.

Miranda nodded in agreement. 'Our experiment for the mystery column competition showed that. That shop is only a whisker away from where we ended up, Holly.'

'So, this is how it could have happened,'

Holly began. 'Kane grabs the money and runs for it.'

'He shoots off down the nearest side-road,' said Miranda.

'Just like I did,' said Holly. A thought occurred to her. 'And if he didn't know the area, he probably went round in a circle like I did, too.'

Peter took up the thinking. 'After running for five minutes or so, he's getting worried. And a bit tired . . .'

'Well, I definitely was,' said Holly.

'So,' Peter continued, 'he ducks into that alleyway to get his breath back. And what does he see? Harry's One-Stop, in the middle of being built.'

'He decides to hide the money and come back to get it later. When the heat's off,' said Peter.

'Except that he never gets to come back,' said Miranda. 'Until now, that is.'

'It was early evening,' said Holly. 'All the workers would have gone off home, but the place would have been wide open.'

'No locks on the doors,' said Peter.

'Probably no doors!' said Miranda.

'And with the floorboards only half laid. It

would have taken him no time at all to stash the money.'

'And when the builders came back first thing next morning,' said Peter, 'they'd have carried on laying the floor where they'd left off. By the time anybody turned up to search the place it would have looked as though nothing *could* have been hidden there.'

Holly nodded thoughtfully. 'And now he's back, pretending to be a council inspector. He's going to be let in and given enough time to pull the floorboards up, recover the money . . .'

'And put the floorboards back again!' cried Miranda. 'It will look as though he's never been there. Talk about the perfect crime!'

The three friends looked at one another. They each knew what the others were thinking. Could the Mystery Kids stop Ginger Kane from getting his hands on the ransom money?

'We have to go to the police,' said Miranda. She looked at the other two. 'Don't we?'

Peter shook his head slowly. 'Would they believe us? I mean, they must have searched all over for that money. Would they think we really knew?'

'They would if . . .' Holly paused. 'If we called them just as Ginger Kane was about to find it.'

'What?' said Peter. 'How on earth can we do that?'

'By being there when he does it,' said Holly.

Miranda's mouth fell open. 'There? In that shop? You're barmy!'

'No, I'm not,' said Holly. 'Peter, is there another way into the shop?'

'Ye-es,' said Peter, unsure what Holly was driving at. 'There's the storeroom door. It leads out to the alleyway.'

'Is it locked?'

Peter shrugged. 'I think so. The key's always in the lock, though. It certainly was this morning.'

'Perfect!' said Holly.

'Perfect?' said Miranda. 'Holly, what are you on about?'

Holly explained. 'How about if one of us unlocked that door tomorrow, before Ginger Kane turns up?'

'One of us?' said Miranda. 'One of you, you mean.'

'OK,' said Holly. 'If I unlocked that door.'

Peter shook his head. 'How would you get in there without Harry seeing you?'

'You and Miranda would have to create a diversion.'

'What, throw a fit or something?' said Miranda, rolling her eyes.

'Anything. It doesn't matter. I'll unlock the door, let myself out, then lock it up again.'

'Then what?'

'Then we keep watch until Ginger Kane turns up. We give him time to start work. Then one of us—'

'*You*,' Miranda interrupted.

'I,' said Holly, 'let myself in through that door and watch to see what he's doing.'

'What if he hears you?' Miranda objected.

'Miranda, he'll be pulling up floorboards. My dad did that last year and, believe me, it is *not* a quiet job. I can be in and out before he knows it. And *then* we can call the police.'

Peter and Miranda looked at each other, then back at Holly.

'Are you sure?'

'Sure I'm sure,' said Holly. 'Just so long as we can get the key to that storeroom door.'

The key

'Are you absolutely sure this is going to work?' whispered Miranda, trying to push herself flat against the wall of the alleyway.

Holly peered over the top of a dustbin. 'Of course it's going to work,' she whispered back. 'What can go wrong?'

Miranda pulled a face. 'I don't know. That's the trouble.'

'If that key is in the basement door like Peter said, then there's no danger.'

'Ah,' said Miranda. 'That's it, then. That's what can go wrong.'

'What?'

'Peter.' Miranda leaned away from the wall and peered round the end. The door to Harry's One-Stop clicked shut as a customer left, clutching a newspaper and a few groceries. 'Shouldn't he be here by now?'

'Yes – *eek*!' Holly stifled a scream as she felt

a hand land on her shoulder.

Holly spun round. 'Peter! Where did you come from?'

'I came through the alleyway from the other end. Sorry, I didn't mean to make you jump.'

'Have you got them?' said Holly.

Peter nodded. Over his shoulder was a bright orange paper-delivery bag. He dipped a hand into the bag and pulled out the walkie-talkies.

'Correction,' groaned Miranda. '*That* is what can go wrong. Them.'

'They've got fresh batteries in,' said Peter.

'Miranda,' said Holly as she clipped one of the handsets to her belt, 'they're perfect for keeping in touch while we're watching out for Ginger Kane. You know they are.'

'Just keep them away from me then,' said Miranda. She bit her lip nervously. 'Are you positively, positively sure this is going to work?'

Holly took a deep breath. 'I'm sure. Come on. It's time to go.'

'I've finished my round, Harry,' said Peter, swinging open the door to the One-Stop.

Behind him, Miranda and Holly drifted in

and began to scan the new arrivals on the magazine rack.

'Good.' Harry checked his watch nervously. 'I . . . er . . . good.' He looked in Holly and Miranda's direction. 'I'll be shutting soon,' he called.

'There was just one thing,' said Peter. 'I put a *Herald* into one house, but I thought they'd cancelled. Can you check?'

Behind the counter, Harry looked at his watch. 'Not now, Peter. Can't it wait until Monday?'

Peter shrugged. 'If you say so. It was number eleven Asquith Crescent, though. . .'

'Oh, no,' groaned Harry. 'I've been arguing with them about their bill all week, you know I have. Oh – just a quick look, then.'

With a sigh, Harry went to the far end of the counter. He bent down to dig out his large newspaper deliveries book.

As he did, Holly slipped quickly past the other end of the counter, through the connecting door and into the storeroom.

The first part of the plan had worked perfectly.

The storeroom was large and gloomy. A

small, barred window of frosted glass let in the only light there was. Holly's heart skipped a beat as she almost knocked over a pile of magazines that she hadn't seen.

She paused, waiting for her eyes to become accustomed to the gloom. Slowly she began to make out shapes round her. More piles of magazines and old newspapers. Cans of this and boxes of that. And more.

It seemed that Harry didn't just use the storeroom for stock. Over on the far side of the room she could see what looked like a collection of ancient office furniture: a filing cabinet, a desk and, in one corner, a large metal cupboard.

Holly moved across to the door. She breathed a sigh of relief.

The key was in the lock!

Murmurings from the shop told her that Harry was still searching for Peter's false cancellation. Slowly, Holly inched her way towards the door.

OK, she told herself. *Unlock the door, take the key, go out, lock the door again. Simple.*

One turn, that was all it would take. Holding her breath, Holly reached out, gripped the key, and turned. It didn't budge!

She tried again. Still the key wouldn't move. The door wouldn't unlock!

Then, suddenly, she heard footsteps outside. Through the frosted glass window she could just make out the shape of a man – a man with a grey raincoat.

She pressed herself against the wall. Who was it?

The man outside was trying to look through the window, bringing his face closer and closer to it as he tried to see through the frosted glass. It was Ginger Kane!

Ducking down low, Holly scuttled beneath the window, round the side of a large cardboard box and then hid behind the old filing cabinet.

She peeped out. The handle of the door was turning. *Thank goodness it's locked*, Holly said to herself.

Moments later, Holly realised why she hadn't been able to unlock that door. It was *already* unlocked.

Before her horrified eyes, the storeroom door swung silently open.

'She should be outside by now,' Miranda hissed in Peter's ear.

'Well, I haven't got any cancellation in here,' said Harry, thumping his newspaper orders book closed.

'Fine. Thanks, Harry,' said Peter.

The shopkeeper checked his watch again. 'Anyway, if there's a problem we'll sort it out another time. Right, now you'd better be on your way.'

He followed them to the door and flipped over the 'OPEN' sign to 'CLOSED'.

'Bye, Harry,' said Peter, following Miranda out.

Harry looked back into the shop. 'Didn't three of you come in?'

'Ah . . . er,' said Miranda, '. . . that was Holly. She – she went out while you were looking in your book.' She hooked her arm round Peter's and pulled hard. 'Byeee!'

'Right,' said Peter, as he and Miranda crossed the road so that they were directly opposite the alleyway. 'Now, it's time for all-round surveillance. Holly should have come out by now. She should be in position at the other end of the alleyway.'

He pulled his walkie-talkie handset from his pocket. 'Now if this doesn't prove to you how useful these are, Miranda, nothing will.'

As Miranda tutted and rolled her eyes, Peter switched on the handset and pressed the talk button. 'MK-one to MK-two. Confirm your position, MK-two. Holly, where are you?'

Holly was in no position to answer.

As the door swung open and Ginger Kane stepped into the storeroom she switched the walkie-talkie handset to OFF. The last thing she wanted was for Peter to be calling her now!

Holly tried to piece things together. What was going on? Why hadn't the storeroom door been locked as Peter had said it would be? Surely if Harry thought Kane was a man from the council, wouldn't he want to show him in himself?

A voice from the other side of the storeroom told her the answer to that question.

'Come on,' she heard Harry say. 'It's all clear.'

She leaned out from her hiding-place as the man in the grey raincoat walked across the storeroom floor. Harry had come in from the shop. 'Where do you want to look?' Holly heard him say. His voice was shaking.

'Over there,' said Kane, pointing to a tall pile of boxes in the far corner of the storeroom. 'I've been waiting a long time for this, you know. Ten long years.'

'You're sure about all this?' Harry said.

'Sure as I can be,' said the man in the raincoat. 'Everything I've found out points to it. And after what you told me yesterday . . .'

Holly had heard enough. Ginger Kane – and Harry. They were in it together!

'She's not answering,' said Peter, staring at the handset.

'I can hear that,' snapped Miranda. 'Or rather I can't hear that.'

'Maybe she's changed the channel setting by accident.'

Peter twiddled with the switch on the front of the handset and tried again.

'Something must have gone wrong,' he said. He looked undecided for a moment, then seemed to make up his mind. 'I'm going round there.'

'Peter!'

'Just to check the storeroom door. She might be stuck or something.'

'What about me?'

'You stay here and keep an eye on the shop. We need to know when Ginger Kane has gone in.'

He started across the road, then came back and handed over his walkie-talkie handset to Miranda. 'Here. Keep trying her.'

'Keep trying her?' As Peter dived across the road and down the alleyway, Miranda looked at the handset in panic. 'How?'

In the storeroom Holly was asking herself what she should do. Wait until they started pulling up floorboards and looking for the money – or try to run for it now?

Suddenly, her mind was made up for her. From outside in the alleyway there came a muffled shout and the sound of scuffling feet. Moments later another man had burst into the storeroom and slammed the door shut.

And he wasn't alone. Held tight in the man's grip was – Peter!

Then a voice shouted. 'Police! Hold it there, Kane!'

It came from the other side of the room. From the man in the grey raincoat!

'No, *you* hold it, Jenkins! One false move and the kid gets hurt. I mean it.'

Jenkins? The man in the grey raincoat – the one they'd been watching all this time – his name was Jenkins?

The snippet from the newspaper. What had it said? 'Kane was arrested by an off-duty policeman. PC Alan Jenkins . . .'

Suddenly, Holly saw it all. Jenkins's picture had been in the paper not because he was Ginger Kane, but because he was the policeman who'd *arrested* him! The Mystery Kids had been following the wrong man – while he had been following . . .

The bobble-hatted man with the clipboard! The man who'd been talking to Harry while Jenkins had been watching from his car. The man Miranda had nearly run over by the woolly jumpers just before they had spotted Jenkins in the market. The man – yes, the bobble-hatted man with the clipboard who'd hurried down Pollards Lane while they were in the electronics shop.

The man Holly was looking at now, who'd grabbed Peter somehow, and was using him as a shield! A man whose bobble hat had been knocked off in the struggle to reveal a thick mass of ginger hair!

Ginger Kane!

'Kane,' said Jenkins, moving towards the man holding Peter, 'I nabbed you once. I'll do it again . . .' He stopped dead as Kane put his free hand into his pocket and pulled out a gun.

'Don't try it, Jenkins, or the kid gets hurt. Now move . . .' He gestured out towards the shop. 'Slowly. This isn't a pea-shooter.'

'Kane, let the kid go.'

'Not until I get what I came for,' said Kane, still holding Peter tight as he followed them across the storeroom. 'Just act sensible, and nobody will get hurt.'

Holly ducked down quickly, almost putting her hand down on a mouse-trap. She heard the snap of a key in a lock. Then footsteps, fading as Ginger Kane led the others out into the front of the shop.

From the shop, she heard the blackmailer barking out orders. 'Empty your pockets. Come on, Jenkins. I know you've got a two-way radio.'

Holly heard the sound of things being put on the shop counter.

'Right. On the floor. Not you, kid. Get one

of those clothes lines, there. Right, now tie
'em up.'

Crawling on all fours, Holly edged out
slightly from her hiding-place until she could
just see through the connecting door and into
the shop. Everybody had their backs to her.
Harry and Jenkins, the policeman, were lying
face down on the floor behind the counter.
Kane had his gun trained on them. Peter, with
one of Harry's clothes lines in his hands, was
bending down.

'Tie 'em good, kid,' Holly heard Ginger
Kane growl. 'Nice and tight. Hands and feet.
Good. Now, go sit over there. And don't
move a muscle. Or else!'

Holly watched as Peter stood up and
walked slowly out of view.

It was her last chance. Any moment now
Kane would be coming into the storeroom
and starting to rip up floorboards. She'd be
discovered for sure. She had to escape, to
find Miranda and go for help. All she had
to do was unlock the storeroom door and
she'd be out into the alleyway before Kane
knew it . . .

She looked across at the door – and her
heart sank. She wasn't going anywhere.

The lock was empty. Kane had removed the key. She was trapped!

'Come in, Holly! Holly, come in!'

Where was she? Why wasn't she answering?

Miranda twisted the channel knob on the handset and pressed the talk button.

'Come in, Holly!'

And where was Peter? Why hadn't *he* come back?

Miranda pressed the talk button and twiddled the channel knob.

'Come in, Holly!

What was going on? Should she go for help?

But if she did, what would she say? 'My friends are looking for a crook who's looking for some money – we think'?

What on earth was she going to do? *If only I could get some answer out of this wretched walkie-talkie*, she thought. *That would be a start*.

Glaring at the handset, Miranda furiously twiddled the channel selector with one hand while pressing the talk button with the other.

'Holly! Come in, Holly! Oh, Holly, where are you?'

Trapped!

Holly was in a jam. She couldn't get out through the storeroom door. And she could hardly run through the shop and get out that way.

Or could she?

From somewhere in the shop came a series of loud thumps, then the sound of splintering wood. Ginger Kane must have started prising up the floorboards in the shop first.

If she could crawl out to the shop door while he wasn't looking . . .

Once again, Holly began to ease herself out from her hiding-place. Further and further, until she was able to stand up.

Slowly, she tiptoed out towards the shop. Nearer and nearer. She needed to know where Kane was. She leaned out slightly – and her eyes met Peter's!

He was sitting on the floor, where Kane

111

had told him to, his back against the maga-zine rack.

As Peter's eyes grew wide, Holly put her finger to her lips. The last thing she wanted now was for him to make a sound. Or did she?

Peter's walkie-talkie handset wasn't on his belt. That could only mean one thing. He'd left it with Miranda! Could she get a message to her?

Not by speaking, she couldn't. Even whis-pering would be too risky. If Ginger Kane heard her, there'd be no way she could escape.

No, she couldn't speak. But Peter could! He could shout something. Kane might shout something back. If Holly pressed the talk button while they were arguing, there was a chance Miranda would hear them and realise what was going on. She'd be able to run for help.

As Peter looked at her, Holly lifted up the handset so he could see it. 'Shout!' she mouthed, hoping desperately that Peter would be able to read her lips.

For a moment Peter looked uncertain. Then he nodded.

'You can't get away with this, Kane!' he yelled.

Holly stuck her thumb up.

Peter yelled again, 'You hear me, Kane? You'll never get away with it!'

'Shaddup, kid!'

Slowly, Holly's thumb moved to the ON/OFF switch.

'How many floorboards are you going to pull up, Kane?' yelled Peter.

'All of them if I have to. That money's round here somewhere. Now—'

Holly flicked the switch to ON. Quickly she moved her thumb to the talk button.

But not quickly enough.

For, before she had the chance to press it, Miranda's voice rang out loud and clear.

'Holly! Where are you, Holly? Oh, I give up!'

At the sound of Miranda's voice, Ginger Kane swung round. As he saw Holly, he started scrambling to his feet.

'Come here, kid. Come here!'

In a blind panic, Holly turned and raced back into the storeroom. Kane chased in after her, the gun in his hand.

'Give me that walkie-talkie, kid. I won't hurt you.'

Holly backed away, holding the handset out in front of her. Kane followed her, crouching like a panther. 'I said, give that to me.'

Holly looked down at the walkie-talkie handset, then back at Kane.

A nasty smile creased the blackmailer's face. 'Give—'

'Here!' screamed Holly.

With all her might she flung the handset at him. Kane ducked, the handset flying past him to smash against the wall.

Holly leaped towards the old office furniture. As Kane lunged after her, she dived under the desk and slid into the small gap behind the large metal cabinet.

Kane's hand reached round, trying to grab her. Holly shrank right back into the corner. Her back bumped against the wall. She could go no further. Any moment now, Kane would have caught her.

As she moved, her foot kicked against something. She looked down and saw one of Peter's mouse-traps.

Kane was pulling at the cabinet, trying to

drag it out. His fingers were reaching round the sides, stretching towards her.

Without hesitating, Holly snatched up the mouse-trap and held it out . . .

The trap snapped against his fingers and Kane reeled backwards with a scream of pain, dropping his gun. A tower of heavy boxes crashed to the ground as he stumbled into them. Kane fell down, groaning.

It was the chance Holly needed. She leaped out from behind the filing cabinet and dashed back into the shop, slamming the connecting door behind her and ramming its bolts into place.

'Holly! Help me!'

It was Peter. In the commotion he'd started to undo the rope round the policeman's hands.

'Quick!' snapped Jenkins. 'Before he gets away.'

'He can't get away,' said Holly. 'The door out to the alleyway is locked . . .'

She realised she was wrong at once. Yes, the door *was* locked. But Kane had the key. He *could* escape!

As the rope binding his ankles fell away,

Jenkins leaped up and unbolted the connecting door.

'Kane!'

It's too late, Holly thought as she saw the door to the alleyway hanging open and heard the sound of running footsteps. *He's gone*.

Then she heard more footsteps and lots of shouting. The sound of scuffles.

Dodging round the mess in the storeroom, Holly and Peter reached the door and looked out into the alleyway. Ginger Kane had been caught. He was on the ground, his arms pinned down by what looked like a dozen policemen.

'How did they get here?' began Holly.

She was interrupted by the wonderfully familiar sound of Miranda's loudest laugh.

Coming along the alley, she was waving the remaining walkie-talkie high in the air.

'Holly, I did it!' she cried. 'It works!'

'Don't ask me how,' said Miranda as they all gathered together in the shop, 'but I just sort of twiddled this and pressed that and was just about to give up . . .'

'We heard you,' Peter said grimly. 'Loud and clear. Trouble was, so did Ginger Kane.'

'Ah,' said Miranda, 'but then I heard *you*, Holly. When Kane was chasing you.'

Holly thought back. She'd had the walkie-talkie in her hand all the time.

'You must have had your finger on the talk button,' said Miranda. 'Because I heard it all. "Give me that walkie-talkie, kid," ' Miranda said in the deepest voice she could manage, ' "I won't hurt you." Well, that's when I went for the police.'

'Then? Not before?' Holly looked at her. 'But . . . how did they get here so fast?'

'Well, that was the funny thing,' said Miranda. 'I shot round the corner, and there they were. A whole *vanful* of them!'

As Holly sighed with relief, Peter said, 'Well done, Miranda.'

Miranda shrugged and smiled.

'So Shifty's on his way back to jail, is he?'

Peter nodded. 'It looks like it.' He stopped as a horrified look came over Miranda's face. 'What's the matter?'

'Th-there!' she spluttered, pointing to the shop door. 'Kane! He's coming back!'

Holly and Peter swung round. A man with a grey raincoat was just coming through the shop door.

'Miranda,' said Holly. 'We got it a bit wrong. We weren't following Ginger Kane. We were following the policeman who caught him. PC Alan Jenkins . . .'

'Ex-PC Alan Jenkins,' said the man himself, coming over to them. 'Now Detective Sergeant. You know, it had always bugged me that we'd never been able to find that ransom money. But I fancied Kane would come after it, so as soon as he was released I started watching him.'

'The man with the bobble hat and the clipboard,' said Holly. 'Remember, Miranda? You nearly ran him down in the market that day? *He*'s Ginger Kane.'

'He had to look round for a fair bit,' said Jenkins. 'He didn't know Highgate when he dumped the money, so he had to work out exactly where to come. But when he gave Harry that story about being a council officer, I knew this was the place.'

'So when we saw you talking to Harry – you were arranging to come here and wait for Kane?' asked Holly.

Jenkins nodded. He picked up his walkie-talkie, still on the counter where Ginger Kane had made him dump it. 'And call my men into action as soon as Kane found anything. Trouble was, I didn't get the chance!'

'So that's why they were all sitting there waiting!' said Miranda.

'Yes,' said Jenkins. 'Waiting for a call that would never have come if it hadn't been for you.'

Holly beamed at Peter and Miranda. 'We're a team,' she said.

'Another case solved,' Peter said happily.

'Not quite,' said Jenkins. 'We still have to find the ransom money.'

'Over here, Sarge!'

Jenkins looked over to where a policeman was burrowing under the floorboards that Ginger Kane had been working on.

The policeman had dragged a small, dust-covered case into the open.

As they all gathered round Holly noticed that, apart from a small round hole in one of its corners, the case still looked quite new.

'At last,' said Jenkins.

He bent down and wiped the top of the case with his hand. Then, as he carefully snapped back the catches, he turned to Holly, Peter and Miranda.

'Ready?'

'You bet!'

The three friends craned forward as Jenkins slowly lifted the lid.

'Oh, no!'

'I will never forget it,' said Miranda. 'Never, *ever*. All those mice, just sitting there!'

'In the middle of all that money!' laughed Holly and Peter as they recalled the sight that had greeted them when Detective Sergeant Jenkins had opened the case.

'What was left of it, you mean! All those notes, torn to bits to make a comfy little home. Would you believe it!' Miranda hooted loudly.

'Ginger Kane wouldn't have been able to take it to a bank without arousing suspicion anyway,' said Holly.

Miranda looked seriously at her. 'But it *is* still worth something. All those scraps?'

'That's what my mum says,' nodded Holly. 'So long as there's enough of a banknote left to identify it, then it can be exchanged for a new one.'

'Well, she should know,' said Miranda.

'The end of the paper chase,' said Peter.

'Hey – how about that as the title for your mystery column competition?'

'I like it!' said Holly. 'Except that we can't really have a competition now, can we?' She waved the newspaper that Peter had brought with him. Splashed across the front page were details of the story, complete with pictures and a map. 'I mean, everybody knows the answer now!'

'And who's won the prize?' said Miranda. 'The Mystery Kids!'

Holly looked at her. 'We have?'

Miranda gave a dramatic sigh. 'Holly Adams, don't you ever read the newspapers?'

She spread out that day's *Highgate Herald* on the floor. They all knelt down around it as Miranda pointed to the small paragraph at the end of the story.

'Look. "Ten years ago, a reward was offered for information leading to the recovery of the money," said a spokesman. "As the money was never found, the reward was never paid out. It looks now as though it *will* be." Get that?' cried Miranda. 'A reward! To the Mystery Kids!'

She put on her most serious look. 'What shall we spend it on?'

'How about—' began Peter.

'I know,' groaned Miranda. 'Don't tell me. Another walkie-talkie to take the place of the one Holly smashed trying to brain Ginger Kane.'

Peter shook his head. 'No, you're wrong. I wasn't thinking of another walkie-talkie.'

'You *weren't*?' said Miranda.

'No,' said Peter, breaking into a broad grin. 'I was thinking of another *two* walkie-talkies. That way we could have one each!'

'*Yes!*' cried Holly. 'Peter, that's a brilliant idea!'

'Then we could carry out three-way surveillance,' said Peter. 'Triangulation, they call it . . .'

'And all talk at the same time,' said Holly.

'OK, so the equipment's a bit more complicated, but not too tricky.'

'Oh, we'd get the hang of it, no problem,' said Holly. 'Wouldn't we, Miranda?'

She turned to look at her best friend.

'Miranda? Why are you banging your head on the floor?'

The Empty House

Fiona Kelly

Hodder
Children's
Books

a division of Hodder Headline plc

The Empty House
Special thanks to Allan Frewin Jones

First published in Great Britain as a single volume in 1995
by Hodder Children's Books

Contents

The new house

'Help!' Holly Adams yelled, as the heavy weight came thumping down on top of her. It knocked her off her feet and flattened her on the stairs. 'Help! I'm being *crushed*!'

She struggled under the suffocating weight, finally managing to drag herself up above the end of the mattress. Her long brown hair was over her face.

Lower down the stairs, her two friends were doubled up with laughter.

'I told you to watch where you were going,' said Peter Hamilton. Miranda Hunt, her long blonde hair tied back with an elastic band, was leaning against the banister rail, helpless with laughter.

'Calm down, you three,' Mr Hamilton said from the hallway. 'We don't want any accidents.' He was carrying the television set.

1

'I think we've just had one,' said Peter. 'You OK, Holly?'

'Miranda did that on purpose!' said Holly. 'I said *stop*!'

'Sorry,' said Miranda, her round face split by a grin. 'I thought you said *shove*!'

'Just you be careful,' said Mr Hamilton. 'I'm beginning to wish I'd hired professional removal men, after all.' He carried the television set into the sitting-room.

The Hamiltons were moving house.

Holly, in her usual way of wanting to be in on everything, had volunteered herself and Miranda to help with the move.

Holly and Miranda were best friends. Both twelve years old, they had lived in the same part of North London all their lives. Peter, on the other hand, had only moved into the area a few months ago. He and his father had been renting a small flat. Now they were finally moving into a house of their own.

Or they *would be*, if the three friends could manage to get Peter's mattress up the stairs to his bedroom.

'OK,' said Peter, hoping that just this once the two girls might follow his instructions. 'Let's try this again, shall we?'

Holly grabbed the top of the mattress.

'Right,' she puffed. 'When I say shove – *shove!*'

'Got you,' said Miranda, squeezing in next to Peter as they both lifted the foot of the mattress in their arms.

'Shove!' said Holly.

They shoved. The mattress twisted and bounced as if it had a life of its own.

'Ow!' wailed Holly, as her heel caught on the stairs and she vanished under the mattress for a second time.

Miranda's piercing laugh rang through the empty house.

Holly struggled to get free again. *There are times*, she thought, *when I wish I wasn't so quick to be helpful!*

Peter's bedroom looked like a left-luggage office after a hurricane has struck. There were boxes and bags and suitcases piled all over the floor, and the furniture was all at strange angles and in odd places. But at least everything was finally in there!

As the three friends sat on the floor, eating fish and chips out of newspaper, they could hear bangs and thuds from downstairs.

A couple of Mr Hamilton's friends were help-ing to move the really heavy furniture.

Holly and her two friends were taking a well-deserved break. They had been toiling away all morning and they were tired and dusty and red-faced from their exertions.

'Phew! I needed that!' said Holly, swigging from a Coke can.

'I need a shower,' said Miranda. 'I'm all sticky and horrible.' She plucked at her T-shirt. 'I haven't worked this hard since . . .' She paused, thinking. 'I haven't worked this hard *ever!*' she said. She looked at Peter. 'Next time you move, remind me to be somewhere else.'

'Next time?' said Peter. 'Are you kidding? We're not moving again, ever!' He looked unhappily round at his jumbled possessions. 'It's going to take me weeks to get all this lot back in order.'

'We'll help you,' said Miranda. She pulled a big sheaf of papers out of a box. 'Where does this go?'

'Leave it!' yelled Peter. 'I'll do it. You'll mess up my system.' Peter had three or four big boxes heaped with notebooks and sheaves of closely written paper. He collected

4

car number plates. He also collected coach and bus numbers. He had a whole stack of reference books. The two girls thought he was mad.

Not that Peter had had much time to pursue his hobby since he had encountered the two girls. Not since the three of them had set up the Mystery Kids.

Holly and Miranda had started the club, inspired by a book they had both read called *Harriet the Spy*. Harriet, who lives in New York, spends her time collecting information about the comings and goings of her friends and neighbours. Holly wanted to do something similar. She had an unquenchable thirst for mysteries – but until she, Miranda and Peter had got together, all Holly's mysteries had been in books. These days, real-life mysteries seemed to erupt all around them.

The name had come from a newspaper headline, *Mystery Kids Foil Bank Robbery*. That had been their first adventure.

Holly screwed up the empty fish-and-chip paper. She stood up, stretching her aching limbs.

'The garden won't need much doing to

it,' she said, looking out of the window. Peter's room was on the first floor at the back of the house. The row of terraced houses was on the crest of a hill. The garden, a neat lawn bordered by flower-beds, sloped down to a rickety-looking wooden fence.

Peter looked over her shoulder. 'That's more than you can say about *that* one,' he said. Beyond the fence, the garden of the house directly behind was like a small jungle. The lawn was a mass of overgrown weeds and spiky grass-heads. Rose bushes and masses of rhododendron spread out of control amongst rubbish and debris. The house itself was obviously empty. It looked almost derelict. From her vantage point, Holly could see bare floorboards in the ground floor rooms.

'Who on earth lives there?' said Miranda, coming up behind them. 'There's no furniture or anything. They must eat off the floor.'

'No one lives there,' said Peter.

'I can see that,' said Miranda. 'I was *joking*.'

'It's number fourteen Roseway Road,' said

Peter. 'I saw something about it in the estate agent's window when I was in there with my dad. It's up for auction in a few weeks.'

'Auction?' said Holly. 'What does that mean?'

'It means it's a dump,' said Peter. 'It means no building society or bank is prepared to lend anyone the money for a mortgage. Whoever buys it will have to pay cash, see?'

'Who'd pay cash for a tip like that?' said Miranda.

Peter shrugged. 'Someone who's prepared to spend a lot of money on it and then sell it off, I suppose,' he said.

'And someone who's prepared to do a lot of work on the garden, too,' said Holly. 'Crumbs! You'd need a flame-thrower to get through that lot!' She stared across at the dusty, uncurtained windows. 'They'd need to clear out all those boxes as well.'

'What boxes?' said Peter.

'Those boxes,' said Holly, pointing towards a pair of glass-panelled doors at the back of the house. Planks and hunks of hardboard were piled against the outside of the doors, but through the glass a group of medium-sized boxes could be seen, stacked together on the floorboards.

'That's funny,' said Peter. 'They weren't there yesterday.'

'Maybe someone's moving in,' said Miranda.

'They can't be,' said Peter. 'I told you, the auction's not for two weeks.'

'Whoever moved out last must have left them, then,' said Holly. 'I expect they're empty.'

Peter gave them a puzzled look. 'Dad and I were over here measuring up yesterday evening,' he said. 'I was in here working out where everything would go. I distinctly remember looking over there and thinking I was glad our house wasn't in such a bad state. And there were no boxes there then, I can tell you that.'

'You just didn't see them,' said Miranda.

'I'd have seen them,' Peter said determinedly. 'If I can see them *now*, I'd have seen them yesterday evening.'

'So what?' said Miranda. 'Who cares about a load of old boxes? Someone's just dumped them there.'

'Yes, but who?' said Holly.

'The man in the moon, for all I care,' said

Miranda. 'Peter? Have you finished with us for the day? Is there any chance of me going home and having a shower now?'

'Aren't you even a little bit intrigued?' Holly asked her.

'Intrigued?' said Miranda. 'About empty boxes in an empty house? No, I'm not. I'm tired and dirty and I want to go home and have a good wash and change out of these sticky clothes.'

'You're sure we can't help you unpack?' Holly asked Peter.

'I'm certain,' said Peter. 'I spent two days packing everything in the right order. If I let you two loose on it, it'll be six months before I get my system sorted out again.'

Miranda rolled her eyes. 'You and your weird hobbies,' she said.

'It's not *weird*,' Peter said, probably for the hundredth time. 'It's interesting.'

'If you say so,' said Miranda, rubbing her nose. The disturbed dust of the move had been making her sneeze all morning. 'But right now, all I'm interested in is getting under a shower. Are you coming, Holly? Or are the pair of you going to spend the rest of the afternoon staring at those boxes over there?'

'I'm coming,' said Holly.

They picked their way through Peter's belongings and headed downstairs.

Through the open sitting-room door they saw Mr Hamilton and the two men who had been helping them move sitting on the couch, taking a break.

'We're off now,' Holly said.

'Thanks for all your help,' said Mr Hamilton.

'That's OK,' said Holly. 'Any time!'

'Holly!' said Miranda. 'Don't say things like that!'

Mr Hamilton laughed. 'Don't worry,' he said. 'We'll be staying put for a while.'

'I'm glad to hear it,' said Miranda.

The front door was wedged open and the large van in which they had moved all the Hamiltons' possessions was standing at the kerb.

'It's going to be great,' said Peter, as he walked with them to the end of the path. 'Plenty of room, at last! We've even set aside a small room just for my files and stuff. We're going to put up shelves and everything. I'm going to have my desk in there. I might even get a filing cabinet.'

'I'm sure you'll be very happy together,' said Miranda. 'You and all your files.'

Holly looked at Peter with suddenly glowing eyes. 'You mean an extra room all to yourself?' she said. 'Hey, we could use it for our meetings. It could be like our own office! The Mystery Kids' office!'

'I don't see why not,' said Peter, turning to go back inside.

This was something Holly had always longed for. A special room where they could meet. Not just a bedroom, but a private room where they could hold meetings and discuss things without interruption.

Peter's old bedroom had been too cramped for meeting up on a regular basis. When they met at Holly's house there was always the problem of Jamie, her pest of a younger brother, sticking his nose in. And at Miranda's house there were her irritating older twin sisters to cope with.

Holly and Miranda lived only a few streets away from each other, and as they walked along, Holly was already full of ideas for their new office.

'I tell you what would be really good,' she said. A great big map of London. We could have it up on the wall. And whenever anything happened, we could stick coloured marker pins in it.'

'And we could have one of those charts, like my mum's got in her office,' said Miranda. 'Showing who's supposed to be doing what, and when. And I know where we can get one, too. There's a shop that sells stuff like that in Croftleigh Road. You know, where the market is.'

'Yes, I know it,' said Holly. 'Let's go there right now.'

'Wait a minute,' Miranda said. 'Not *now*, Holly! I'm filthy. Look at me!'

Once Holly's enthusiasm was fired up, it was difficult to stop her. 'But, Miranda—'

'Tomorrow!' interrupted Miranda. 'We can go over there tomorrow. All the shops over there are open on a Sunday. We'll go over there with Peter in the morning, OK?'

Holly frowned. Tomorrow! She didn't want to have to wait until tomorrow. But then she thought how grubby she was herself after a morning of heavy removal work.

'OK,' she said with a smile. 'Tomorrow. And then we can start setting up the office! Brilliant! It'll be absolutely brilliant!'

Midnight torchlight

It was Sunday morning at Holly's house, and Holly was cooking scrambled eggs for the family. She'd found the recipe in a magazine. Eggs, milk, cheese, salt, pepper and chives. Cook until firm and serve on buttered toast.

'It's ready!' cried Holly. Mr and Mrs Adams were at either end of the table, the Sunday papers spread out in front of them. Jamie was busy with a pocket game machine that sent out a constant barrage of high-pitched beeps.

The newspapers were cleared away.

'This looks good,' said Mr Adams with a smile. 'Jamie! Come on, don't let it get cold.'

'What're these bits?' said Jamie, jabbing his finger at the scrambled egg.

'Chives,' said Holly. 'They're nice.'

'They're not,' said Jamie. 'They're horrible. It looks like grass.'

'Eat!' said Mrs Adams sternly. 'If Holly's gone to the trouble of making it for us, you can at least give it a try.'

Jamie mumbled something about sheep food.

'Very nice,' said Mrs Adams. She looked at Holly. 'Are you going over to Peter's house today?'

'Later,' said Holly. 'First of all we're going to Croftleigh Road to pick up some stuff for our office.'

Mr Adams gave her a quizzical look. Holly explained about the spare room in Peter's new house.

'It's amazing,' Mr Adams said with a laugh. 'I spend all my life wishing I *wasn't* in an office, and Holly, here, can't wait to get into one.' Holly's father was a successful solicitor, but his real love was carpentry. He spent most of his free time in his workshop in the cellar.

'Are you sure Peter's father won't mind you invading his house like that?' said Mrs Adams.

Holly shook her head. 'There's plenty of room there,' she said. 'We won't be in the way at all.'

Holly met up with Miranda an hour or so later, and the two of them set off to pick up Peter. The house was still full of unopened boxes, and the buzz of an electric drill sounded from where Peter's father was already busy putting up some shelves.

'Got all your files sorted?' Miranda asked.

'Not yet,' said Peter, as he closed the front door behind them. 'While we're out, Dad wants me to have a look for a second-hand video machine.' He smiled. 'I've been on at him for ages to get one. There's a shop that sells second-hand stuff like that in Croftleigh Road. We can have a look in there.'

The three of them set off for Croftleigh Road. They came out of an alley between two shops and found the small street market right in front of them.

The electrical shop was called Square Deal. The three friends went inside to have a look round. There certainly was a lot of stuff in there: televisions, video recorders, electric typewriters, word processors and mobile phones filled the racks.

A man stood behind a counter at the back of

the shop, doing something to a small portable television set with a tiny screwdriver.

While Peter asked the man about a video, Holly and Miranda browsed among the shelves.

The man showed Peter a few video machines while Peter wrote down the details and prices.

'Well?' asked Miranda as they left the shop. 'Did you see anything?'

'I think so,' said Peter. 'I'll have to report back to Dad, to see how much he wants to spend.'

Their next stop was at the office and stationery suppliers, a little way along the road.

Inside, they found exactly what they wanted: a huge wall map of the whole of London. The major streets were picked out in yellow, parks and open spaces in green. It was over a metre wide and about a metre high. *Exactly* what they wanted.

They pooled their money and bought it, using the little money they had left over for a small box of coloured pins.

'Now we're really in business,' said Holly as she walked along with the map rolled under her arm. 'Let's get back and put it up.'

Holly didn't say so, but she was a little bit disappointed when she saw the size of their new room. It was a tiny boxroom right at the top of the house. Already, Peter's cartons almost filled it.

But at least it was their own room. A place where they could be sure of not being disturbed by her pesky brother and Miranda's sarcastic sisters.

They spent most of the day sorting the room out. At least, Peter did. He wouldn't let the two girls touch his precious files, so they sat round happily chatting about all the things they could get up to in there, while he toiled away.

The map looked very professional up on the wall. Holly put three blue pins in it, marking out the streets where they lived.

'It's a pity we don't have any mysteries to solve right now,' said Miranda, grinning as she watched the way Peter meticulously sorted his files into neat piles on the floor.

'There's always the mystery of why Peter keeps stacks and stacks of number plates,' said Holly.

'Ha, ha,' said Peter. He was used to being laughed at by the two girls, and he didn't really mind.

They arranged to hold their first meeting after school on Monday.

'Maybe by then,' Miranda said to Peter as she and Holly left, 'you'll have got all your stuff out of the way and we'll actually have some room in there.'

Holly and Miranda went to the Thomas Petheridge Comprehensive. Peter had been living in Highgate for only a few months and had been attending a school a long train journey away. But that was going to change very soon. Peter was transferring to Holly and Miranda's school in a couple of weeks' time.

The girls were looking forward to that. Peter had always insisted that the girls shouldn't discuss Mystery Kids work when he wasn't with them. But soon, with Peter at the same school, they would be able to talk about their adventures all the time.

Not that the two girls had any shortage of other things to talk about at school. Especially as they co-edited the lower-school magazine, *The Tom-tom*. It was only a few photocopied sheets which came out monthly, but Holly and Miranda spent an enormous amount of their free time at school vetting articles and coming up with new ideas to make the magazine as interesting as possible.

Peter had his camera in his hand when they arrived at his house on Monday afternoon.

'I've been taking a whole lot of shots of the house,' he told them. 'I'm going to make a before-and-after portfolio, so that we'll be able to see how different the place looks once we've got it all sorted out and decorated.'

They went upstairs, stopping off at his bedroom so he could take a few snaps of the garden out of the window.

'Hey,' said Holly, looking out of the window. 'Those boxes have gone!'

Peter grinned. 'I was wondering if you'd spot that,' he said. 'Come on up to our office. I've got something even more interesting to tell you.'

Peter had pinned a notice on the door of their office:

PRIVATE
STRICTLY OUT OF BOUNDS
NO ENTRY

'Very impressive,' said Miranda. 'I suppose *we're* allowed in, are we?'

'Only if you give the special knock,' said Peter. He rapped his knuckles on the door. *Tap ti-ti tap tap . . . Tap tap!*

Miranda giggled. She often found Peter and Holly's secret agent tactics comical.

Ignoring her, Peter opened the door and they went inside.

Their room was looking a lot tidier. Peter's desk was in there now and his files were all stacked out of the way against the wall.

'There's only one chair,' Miranda pointed out. 'Where are we supposed to sit?'

'You could try the floor,' suggested Peter. 'I'll get some cushions up here later.'

The three of them sat on the floor.

'Well?' said Holly. 'What's the big news?'

'I was lying in bed last night,' Peter said with slow relish. 'I couldn't get off to sleep. I was thinking about how I am going to arrange my files once Dad's put the shelves up in here.'

'That'd put me to sleep in ten seconds flat,' said Miranda.

'*Five* seconds,' added Holly.

'Do you want to hear about this or not?' asked Peter.

'Go on, then,' said Holly. 'You were lying awake last night. Then what?'

'I thought I heard a noise out the back,' said Peter. 'It's really quiet here at night. So I had a look out of my window. And guess what I saw?'

'I know,' said Miranda. 'There was a whole gang of fairies having a barbecue at the bottom of your garden.'

'I saw *lights* in that empty house,' Peter said, ignoring Miranda. 'I don't mean electric lights. Not normal house lights. It looked like torchlight. It sort of came and went, as if someone was creeping about in there.'

'Did you see anyone?' asked Holly.

'Well, yes – sort of,' said Peter. 'That was the really strange bit. It was upstairs. The torchlight was moving round up there, and then there was this sudden flash.' Peter made an explosive gesture with both hands. 'It was only for a split second. A really bright light. And I saw two silhouettes –

22

just for an instant.' He looked at the two girls.

'Wow,' breathed Miranda. 'Did you see anything else?'

'No,' said Peter. 'After the flash of light, the torchlight carried on moving round upstairs for about ten minutes and then it went out. I kept watch for a while longer, but nothing else happened. Except that when I looked out this morning all those boxes were gone.' He looked at the two girls. 'Is that strange, or what?'

'Maybe it's squatters,' said Holly. 'You know, people who saw the house was empty and just moved in illegally.'

'Why would squatters creep about at midnight moving boxes?' said Peter.

'I know,' said Miranda. 'It was a *murder*. Someone lured a victim there. Then he stole all their money, chopped them into little bits and hid them in the boxes.'

'You are the most gruesome person in the *world*!' said Holly. 'You've got a seriously warped mind, Miranda, do you know that?'

Miranda grinned. 'It was just a theory,' she said.

'I don't think it was anything like that,' said

Peter. 'But I think I know what the bright light was. It was a flash-bulb from a camera. I'm sure there's something strange going on over there. And it's got something to do with those boxes.'

'You mean something criminal?' asked Holly. 'Hey, maybe it's a spy ring?' her eyes shone as her imagination started to work. 'I've got it! Some foreign power has sent its top spies over here to gather information. Those boxes are probably full of radio transmitters and bugging devices. And cameras with enormous zoom lenses.'

'Just like in *Spyglass*,' said Miranda. *Spyglass* was their favourite television programme. Every week the Mystery Kids were glued to the screen, breathlessly following the adventures of Secret Agent John Raven. 'They might have long-distance listening devices, too.' She glanced towards the window. 'We'd better keep our voices down. They could be listening to us *right now*!'

'I wouldn't have thought so,' said Peter. 'I can't really see a foreign power sending people all the way over here to listen to *you*.'

'But you agree it *might* be spies?' said Holly.

'Not really,' said Peter. 'But I think we could do some investigating.' He grinned. 'After all, that's what we set up the Mystery Kids for, wasn't it? To investigate strange things like this.'

'What sort of investigating could we do?' asked Miranda. 'If all this goes on at night, I don't see what we can do about it.'

'I'm going to keep watch,' Peter said firmly. 'All night, if I have to.'

'Rather you than me,' said Miranda. 'I bet you fall asleep.'

'I won't!' Peter protested.

'OK,' said Holly. 'You keep watch on the place tonight, Peter. We'll come over here after school tomorrow, and you can fill us in on anything you see.'

'Will do,' said Peter.

'*If* you keep awake,' said Miranda.

'I'll keep awake, all right,' said Peter. 'Don't worry about that! I shan't close my eyes for a *second*!'

3 Footprints in the dust

It was the week in which *The Tom-tom* came out, and, as usual, all Holly and Miranda's spare time at school was being taken up in last-minute preparations for the magazine.

The two girls were in the resource room. Holly was sitting at the word processor while Miranda watched over her shoulder.

'Wouldn't it be quicker if you used more than two fingers?' Miranda asked as Holly tapped at the keyboard.

'It'd be quicker if you weren't breathing down my neck,' said Holly. 'Can't you find something useful to do? Think up a couple of jokes for the funny section.'

'We've got plenty,' said Miranda. Miranda was in charge of the joke page. She picked up a scrap of paper. 'What about this one? What goes black-white-black-white-black-white?'

26

'I don't know,' said Holly, trying to concentrate on her typing.

'A penguin rolling down a hill,' said Miranda.

Holly groaned.

'Have you remembered that notice Mr Taylor gave us?' asked Miranda. Mr Taylor was the head teacher. He frequently used *The Tom-tom* to get information round the school.

'Front page,' said Holly, scrolling the screen back to page one.

'"It's fund-raising time again!"' Holly read.

'"Mr Taylor has asked us to remind you that the official fund-raising campaign starts this week. We are collecting money for some additional computer terminals for the school. Anyone with any brilliant ideas for ways of raising money should contact Miss Springfield in the secretary's office. Come on, you lot, think up some ideas! We need those terminals, and we need them *now*!"'

'That should do the trick,' said Miranda. 'Have you come up with any ideas?'

'Not yet,' said Holly.

'We could kidnap Mrs Jarman and hold her to ransom,' suggested Miranda. Mrs Jarman was a terrifying games teacher. She was known as Queen Kong.

'Who'd pay to get *her* back?' asked Holly. 'People would pay to get *rid* of her, maybe.'

Holly scrolled the screen back to where she had left off and began to type in the results of recent netball matches.

Miranda took out her red pen and did a final edit of the jokes page. One thing *The Tom-tom* was never short of were terrible jokes handed in by the rest of the lower school.

'I wonder how Peter got on last night,' said Holly.

'He'll have fallen asleep,' said Miranda. 'You can bet on it.'

'No he won't,' said Holly. 'Knowing Peter he'll have spent half the night staring out of that window. You know what he's like.'

'Is it a bet, then?' asked Miranda. 'Fifty pence says he was fast asleep by ten o'clock.'

'You're on,' said Holly. 'That'll be the easiest fifty pence I ever make. It can go towards the computer.'

'Fifty pence!' said Miranda with a grin. 'Hand it over, Holly.'

They were in their office in Peter's house that afternoon. The good news was that Peter had brought up some cushions for them to sit on. The bad news, especially for Holly, was that he had admitted falling asleep after about half an hour of watching.

'This moving house business is really exhausting,' Peter explained, his face red with shame. 'I couldn't keep my eyes open.'

'You should have propped them open with matchsticks,' Holly complained. 'That's the last time I trust you!'

'I woke up later,' said Peter. 'There were some cats having a yowling competition. They sound really weird, you know, in the middle of the night. I had a look out of the window.'

'Any lights in the house?' Holly asked hopefully.

'Nope,' said Peter. 'But I could *almost* swear I saw someone moving about in the garden over there. It was dead dark, but I'm sure I saw something move.'

'Yes,' said Miranda. 'Courting cats, I expect.'

'So now what do we do?' asked Holly, frowning at Peter. 'It doesn't look like we can trust you to keep watch.'

'Why don't we just go round there?' suggested Miranda. 'You never know, we might spot something through the front windows. You know, traces of dried blood where the landlord chopped up—'

'Miranda!' exclaimed Holly. 'Will you shut up about that! We're looking for spies, not maniacs with choppers. Murderers don't take photos, for heaven's sake! But you're right about one thing. We ought to go and have a look over there.'

They had put a red pin in the map to show where the empty house was. Red for mystery.

They headed down the street, turning left down the hill and then left again into Roseway Road. It was a street of two-storey houses, smaller and not as old as the house where Peter lived. Round bay windows looked out over narrow front gardens, although many of the gardens had been concreted over or only showed a few shrubs behind their low brick walls.

The empty house was easy to spot. Number fourteen. There was a large sign attached to the gate-post. It read *House for Auction* then the date of the auction and a telephone number for enquiries underneath. Not that it would have been difficult to spot the house, even without the sign. There was rubbish in the front area and the windows were bare of the net curtains which hung across the majority of the other houses' windows.

Someone with green fingers had obviously owned the house at some point, because there was a trellis to one side of the sunken front doorway, and an out-of-control climbing plant hung half-across the entrance, covered in tiny white flowers.

'That's a jasmine plant,' said Miranda. 'It grows like crazy if you don't keep it under control.'

'Anyone got a pair of shears?' asked Peter, as he pushed the hanging tendrils aside and stepped up into the shadowy doorway.

Holly picked her way through the rubbish and peered through the gaping bay window.

'Nothing here,' she said. The room beyond was bare. Holly thought it looked terribly sad. There were dusty floorboards, and cobwebs over the ceiling. Lighter patches showed on the wallpaper where pictures had once hung. A naked bulb hung from the ceiling rose.

'Poor house,' she said. 'It needs a family to bring it back to life.'

She went to join her two friends in the doorway. Peter was trying to see through the door's frosted-glass panels. Two further glass panels were set into the sides of the door frame.

Miranda pushed the doorbell. There was no sound.

'It's probably linked up to the electrics,' said Peter. 'That would all have been cut off when the last people moved out.' He crouched down and pushed at the letterbox. It opened with a creak.

'Anything?' asked Holly.

'A few letters and stuff,' said Peter, angling himself to try and see into the hallway. 'It's probably just junk mail.'

The glass in the side panels was clearer than in the door itself. Holly pulled her sleeve down over her hand, to give the dusty glass a quick wipe in the hope of seeing more clearly.

'Oh, crumbs!' she gasped. As she had pressed the heel of her hand against the glass panel, it had shifted inwards from one side. Holly winced, expecting the whole panel to come crashing down into the hall. But it didn't. It was held by a strip of wood on one side.

'You vandal!' said Miranda. 'I saw you do that!'

'It wasn't *me*,' said Holly. 'I hardly touched it. It was already loose. Someone's taken out the strips of wood that should be holding it in place.' She gave the glass panel a tentative push with her finger and it scraped a little further open, leaving a small gap.

'Anyone could get in,' said Peter. 'All you'd need to do is reach through and I bet you could open the door.'

The three of them looked at one another.

'Should we?' said Holly.

'We could,' said Peter.

'Why not?' said Miranda.

'Isn't it a bit like breaking in?' said Holly. 'I mean, we'd be trespassing.'

'Only if we were caught,' said Miranda. 'And even then, we'd probably only get a good telling-off by the police.'

'Thanks,' said Holly. 'That's a great comfort.'

'You know what they say,' said Peter. *'Who dares wins.'*

Holly gave him a dubious look. 'Who says that?'

'I don't remember,' said Peter. 'But I know *someone* says it. And we're never going to catch any spies if we don't take a few risks.'

Holly looked at him. 'You really think it might be spies?'

'Well, whoever they were, they had a camera,' said Peter. 'And there's only one way to find out what they were up to.'

'Come on,' urged Miranda. 'Let's do it. We could be in and out before anyone saw us. And if there really is something screwy going on in there . . .' Her voice trailed off. She didn't need to say any more. They were all thinking the same thing: strange night-time lights in an empty house was just too good a mystery for the Mystery Kids to ignore.

Miranda didn't wait for any further discussion. She pushed her hand through the narrow gap and a second later the front door creaked open.

'OK,' said Peter. 'In and out as quick as we can, right?'

He pushed the door open and stepped

into the dusty hallway. Bare stairs led up to the top floor. Two doors stood open from the hall.

Miranda sneezed. Holly nearly jumped out of her skin.

'Sorry,' said Miranda. 'I'm allergic to house dust.'

Peter closed the door behind them and pushed the glass panel back into place. 'Just in case,' he said.

'In case of what?' asked Holly.

Peter shrugged. 'In case someone comes by and sees that the door is open,' he said. 'Hey! Look!'

The two girls followed the line of his pointing finger. The floorboards were thick with dust beyond the scattering of unwanted envelopes and local free papers.

'Someone's been in here,' said Holly. They could all see the way the dust had been disturbed. There were no actual footprints, but there were clear scuffings and scrapings in the dust to show that the house had recently been entered.

The trail of disturbed grime led along the hall and out through the furthest open door.

They followed the marks.

'Someone's been upstairs as well,' said Holly.

Peter nodded. 'I told you I saw the lights upstairs, didn't I?' he said.

They followed the marks of passing feet into the back room.

'This is the room you can see from your house,' said Holly. It was an empty room with French windows overlooking the wilderness that had once been a garden.

'No more boxes,' said Miranda, rubbing her nose as the dust of the abandoned house threatened another sneeze. In the filtering sunlight they could see tiny specks of dust hanging in the air.

'Who's for investigating upstairs?' asked Holly.

'We're here now,' said Peter. 'We might as well have a good look round.'

A sound from the hallway froze them where they stood.

In the emptiness of the house, the sound was horribly clear.

The chink and rattle of a key being put in the lock of the front door.

'Can we get out the back way?' whispered Holly.

They tiptoed towards the French windows. Holly had her fingers on the door handle when the tickling in Miranda's nose became too much for her.

'*Atishoo!*' sneezed Miranda. 'Oh, crumbs! Sorry! *Atishoo!*'

Holly and Peter stared at her in horror.

'Who's there?' shouted a voice from the hallway.

The three friends stared at one another. They were well and truly caught!

4 Now you see it, now you don't

A smartly dressed young woman came storming into the back room of the old house. Her blonde hair was cut severely short and her piercing blue eyes stared at the three friends from behind red-framed spectacles. She was carrying a large bunch of keys in one hand and a briefcase in the other.

The clicking of her heels came to an ominous stop as she regarded Holly and her friends with knitted eyebrows.

'How did you get in here?' she demanded.

'Through the front door,' said Holly, her heart sinking. She already had visions of being marched off to the police station. Her mother would have plenty to say about *that*, she was sure. 'We weren't doing any harm,' she added.

'How dare you break in here,' said the woman. 'This is private property.' Her icy stare was unnerving. 'Do you know what that means?'

'Of course we do,' Miranda said fearlessly. 'We were only having a look round. And we didn't break anything to get in here, either.'

Good old Miranda, thought Holly. *She's not scared of anything.* And what she said was true enough – they hadn't broken anything. The glass pane had already been loosened.

'Do you mean the front door wasn't locked?' asked the woman. 'Is that what you're telling me?'

'I just pushed the door,' said Peter. 'And it came open.' That was true. Peter had pushed the door open after Miranda had unlocked it.

Holly was about to mention the loose panel when Peter continued. 'Whoever owns this place ought to be more careful about security,' he said. 'Anyone could have got in.'

'Is this your house?' asked Miranda.

'No,' said the woman. 'I work for the estate agent.' The severity of her expression had softened a little. 'You had no business being in the doorway in the first place,' she said.

'Sorry,' said Holly. 'We saw the place

was empty. We didn't think anyone would mind.' She nodded towards Peter. 'He saw this place mentioned in the estate agent's office. His father was looking for a house. We just thought we'd come and check this one out.'

'That's not the way to go about it,' said the woman. 'You should have made an appointment. I can't just have people wandering in and out of properties when they feel like it.'

'Sorry,' said Peter. 'We didn't realise.'

Whatever the woman had intended to say next was interrupted by a hammering on the front door.

'Hello? Hello in there!' A man's voice. Footsteps sounded down the hall and an elderly man appeared in the doorway.

'Are you from the estate agent's?' the man demanded. He gave the three friends a brief glance before focusing his eyes on the woman. 'I've been wanting to catch you for weeks. I demand to know how long it is going to take for this property to be sold. It's an eyesore. What are you doing about it, eh?'

'And you are?' asked the woman.

'Frazer. Sidney Frazer. I own the house next door,' said the man. 'Do you realise this property has been empty for over six months? That garden out there is completely out of control. It's a disgrace.' He glared at the three friends. 'And what are these children doing in here? Causing mischief, I expect.'

'No, we aren't,' said Miranda.

'Children are always causing mischief,' said the old man. 'Or *worse*. There have been a lot of burglaries round here recently.' He stared meaningfully at the three. 'Mrs Milligan at number twenty-three was burgled only last week.'

'We're not burglars!' Miranda snapped. 'What kind of an idiot burglar would come into an empty house? We were just having a look round.'

'Exactly!' said Mr Frazer. 'And that's what happens when houses are left empty. They attract undesirables!'

Miranda glared at the unpleasant old man. 'Can we go now?' she said. 'I don't think this is the sort of street Peter and his father would want to live in anyway.'

'Yes,' said the woman. 'Go! And don't

let me catch you anywhere near this place again, or you'll be in real trouble.' She looked at Peter. 'If your father wants to view this property, he will have to make an appointment.'

'I don't think he'll bother,' said Peter. 'He wants a place with friendly neighbours. Thanks all the same.'

Mr Frazer made a 'harrumph' noise as they walked past him.

Holly and her friends were surprised to see yet another man at the front door. A man in his twenties, wearing overalls. He was staring at the open door with a puzzled, uneasy look on his face.

'What are you lot doing in here?' said the man. Before they had time to answer, the estate agent came marching into the hall, her heels clicking.

'Can I help you?' she asked.

The man looked past the three friends. 'I'm from the electricity board,' he said. 'I've come to read the meter.'

'Don't be ridiculous,' said the woman. 'The electricity was cut off in this property six months ago.'

Holly could tell from the way the man's

eyes shifted that he was doing some speedy thinking.

'Is this fourteen Acacia Road?' he said.

'Fourteen *Roseway* Road,' said the woman.

'I've got the wrong place,' said the man.

'So it would seem,' said the woman. 'Acacia Road runs parallel to this one, further down the hill.'

'Thanks,' said the man. 'Sorry to bother you.' He made a hasty retreat, got into a car and drove away.

Holly led her friends out from under the dangling jasmine. As they came to the pavement, they heard Mr Frazer speaking.

'I want something done about the garden, and I want it done *now*.'

'What a lovely person to have as a next-door neighbour,' said Miranda. 'I bet you're glad you're not moving in here, Peter.'

Holly waited until they were out of earshot of the house.

'He wasn't from the electricity board,' she said. 'They drive around in official vans. He was just in an ordinary car.'

'So who was he?' asked Peter.

'I think it's time we went back to our office and had a proper think about this,' said Holly. She thought she sounded very professional.

'We talked our way out of trouble pretty well back there,' Miranda said as they walked along. 'Don't you think we should have told her about the loose panel, though?'

'I was going to when Peter interrupted me,' said Holly.

'Look,' said Peter. 'If we'd told her, she'd have got it fixed, wouldn't she?'

'I suppose she would,' said Holly.

'And then whoever's creeping about the house in the middle of the night wouldn't be able to get in, would they?' said Peter. 'Our mystery would be over almost before it began. You know what it's like once adults get involved. This is *our* mystery, and we're going to solve it.'

'Good thinking, Sherlock,' said Miranda. 'Why give up a good mystery without a fight?'

Peter grinned. 'You mean you agree with me?' he said.

'Of course,' said Holly. 'Don't look so surprised.'

44

'But you two hardly ever agree with anything I say,' said Peter.

'We do when you're right,' said Miranda. 'Can we help it if you're not right very often?'

They took a quick detour to the chemist's on their way back to Peter's house, so that he could pick up the photographs he had taken of his new home.

'OK,' said Holly, once they were safely behind the closed door of their office. 'Let's think this through. Boxes appear in an empty house, and then vanish in the middle of the night. That same night, Peter sees lights in the house. And the flash óf a camera. A man turns up at the house, pretending to be from the electricity board, and does a disappearing act as soon as he sees there are people there.' She was writing in her notebook as she spoke. 'I'm going to call that fake meter reader Sparky,' she said. She wrote it down. *Code-name: Sparky*.

'I wish we knew what was in those boxes,' said Miranda.

'There's definitely something peculiar going on in there,' said Holly. 'I'm more convinced than ever, now. It may not be a spy ring,

45

but I'll bet it's something sneaky. Something that no one is supposed to know about.'

'It's a pity we got caught before we could have a proper look round,' said Miranda. 'Peter, you said the lights were upstairs, didn't you? Ahem, Peter! Are you paying attention?'

Peter looked up from flipping through his photographs. 'Yes,' he said. 'I'm listening.'

'Well?' asked Miranda.

'Well what?' asked Peter. 'Sorry, I was just – oh! That's odd. Take a look at this.'

He held out one of the photographs to the girls. It was a shot of the back garden, taken from his bedroom window. In the top half of the photograph, the overgrown garden beyond the back fence was visible, as well as a section of the empty house.

'Yes,' Holly said drily. 'Very nice.'

Peter grinned. 'You haven't spotted it, have you?' he said. 'Oh! Of course! You haven't looked out of my bedroom window recently.' He got up. 'Come with me,' he said. 'I want to show you something.'

They went to his room and stared out of the window.

'OK,' said Miranda. 'What are we looking at?'

Holly looked from the photograph to the view out of the window. Peter had seen something. It was like one of those puzzles where you get two pictures side by side and have to discover ten differences between them.

'Got it!' shouted Holly. 'In the photo there's a lot of stuff piled up against the French windows, but the stuff isn't piled up there now.'

'Oh, yes,' said Miranda. 'It's all on the grass. I see. So someone has used those French windows recently.'

'Didn't I tell you I thought I saw someone in the garden the other night?' said Peter. 'That proves it. And look, in the photo the door to that garden shed is open. But it's closed now. Someone has been in the shed.'

It was true. Over to one side of the garden stood a ramshackle old shed. In the photograph, the door was hanging wide open. But as they looked out of the window, they could see that the shed door was now tightly closed and held by an angled length of wood.

'Right,' said Holly, her eyes shining with excitement. 'That's our next job, then. To find out what's been going on in that garden!'

5 Breaking in

'We can't risk going back in that house,' said Peter. 'You heard what the woman said. We'd be in big trouble if she caught us round there again.'

Miranda nodded in agreement. 'She's not going to believe we're just having a look round again,' she said. Her face brightened. 'Unless we go over there in disguise!'

'What sort of disguise?' said Peter. 'We're still going to look like twelve-year-olds whatever we do. Unless you fancy wobbling over there on stilts and wearing a long coat. How do you think I'd look in a false moustache?'

'Even dopier than you look right now,' said Miranda. 'And I don't suppose dark glasses and big hats would fool anyone, either. You know, there are times when it's a real *pain* being young! If we were grown-up we could just put on wigs and funny voices and go round there pretending we wanted to buy the place.' She jumped up. 'Good afternoon,' she said in a deep voice. 'My name is Mrs Twitterington-Smythe.' She made a grand gesture towards Peter. 'And this is my butler, Perkins. I'd like to arrange to view number fourteen Roseway Road, my good woman. And hurry up about it, I'm having tea with the Lord Mayor this evening!'

Peter shook his head. 'You're batty,' he said.

'When you two have quite finished,' said Holly, 'I'd like to say something.'

Miranda sat down. 'Mrs Twitterington-Smythe is all ears,' she gurgled.

'We don't have to go into the house again,' said Holly. 'All we need to do is hop over the back fence.'

'What?' said Peter. 'In broad daylight? With that estate-agent woman still lurking around? Not to mention the nosy neighbour from next door. They'd be all over us before we could move.'

'I wasn't thinking we should do it right now,' said Holly. 'We could do it tomorrow afternoon.'

'But we'll be seen!' exclaimed Peter.

'Maybe,' Holly said coolly. 'Which is why we need to come up with a reasonable excuse.'

'I know,' said Miranda. 'We could tell them we're practising for the inter-school hurdles championship. You know, leaping garden fences as part of our training routine.'

'Tennis,' said Holly. '*That's* our excuse. We can have a game of tennis in Peter's garden tomorrow afternoon. We could accidentally-on-purpose lob the ball over the back fence. No one could blame us for hopping over the fence to look for our ball, could they?' She looked at her two friends. 'Well?' she said. 'What do you say?'

'I can't play tennis,' said Peter.

'That's no problem,' said Holly. 'The ball's even more likely to get lost if you don't know what you're doing.'

'I haven't got a racket,' added Peter.

'I'll lend you one,' said Miranda. 'And don't worry, with my brilliant power serve, that ball will be over the fence like a rocket!'

'Ow!' Peter yelled as the tennis ball bounced

off the back of his head. 'I wasn't ready for it yet! I was doing up my shoelace!'

Miranda gave a shriek of laughter. 'It wouldn't have made any difference if you *were* ready,' she yelled. 'You haven't hit one ball since we've been out here!'

It was the following afternoon. Holly and Miranda had arrived at Peter's house with their rackets after school. The sun blazed down as the two girls ran rings round Peter. He had been right about one thing – he couldn't play tennis.

'Mr Hamilton to serve,' said Holly, who was temporary umpire. 'Miss Hunt leads two games to love in the first set. New balls, please.'

'We've only got one ball,' Miranda reminded her.

'I know,' said Holly. 'But you're supposed to say "new balls, please" every now and then. It's how they do it on the telly. Peter, for heaven's sake, hold the racket properly. Anyone would think it was a *snake*, the way you're holding it!'

'Don't keep on at me,' complained Peter. 'I'm doing my best. How do I serve again?'

'Chuck the ball in the air and wallop it,'

said Miranda. She bounced professionally from foot to foot in her white shorts and white T-shirt, her long hair flying.

Peter hurled the ball into the air and made a futile swipe at it. The two girls rocked with laughter as the ball fell unwalloped at his feet.

He threw his racket down.

'Misuse of racket,' yelled Holly. 'Game violation by Mr Hamilton. One point penalty. Love fifteen.'

'Oh, shut up,' said Peter. 'I'll be umpire. You two play. I thought the whole idea was to get that ball over the fence, not to make me look a complete idiot.'

'We can do both,' laughed Miranda. 'No problem.' She moved down to the bottom of the garden and Holly prepared to serve.

The ball bounced and arched into the air.

Miranda leaped into the air and returned the ball with a yell of triumph.

'You can't get past the mighty Hunt!' she said.

'You twit,' said Holly. 'That would have gone over the fence!'

'Oh! Sorry!' said Miranda. 'I got carried away.'

'Just *leave* it next time,' said Holly. She served again, a much lower lob that bounced almost at Miranda's feet. Miranda ducked to avoid it, and the ball sailed over the fence.

'Oh dear,' said Miranda. 'We seem to have lost our ball!'

'About time!' said Peter. 'Can we get on with it, now?'

They headed down to the bottom of the garden. Peter tested the strength of the fence. It wobbled alarmingly.

'It's going to collapse if we're not careful,' he said.

'Never!' said Holly. 'You're always looking for problems, Peter.' She bounced on her toes a couple of times, grabbed the top of the shoulder-high fence and hauled herself up on to it.

There was a creaking, cracking noise.

'Holly, careful!' wailed Miranda.

But it was too late. With a loud crunching noise, an entire section of the fence broke away from its supporting posts and deposited Holly on her face in the adjoining garden.

'Brilliant!' said Peter. 'Absolutely brilliant,

Holly! Thanks a lot. My dad will be really pleased when he gets home and sees this.'

Holly picked herself up, brushing splinters of rotten wood off her clothes. 'It's OK, Peter,' she said. 'Don't worry. I haven't hurt myself. Thanks for asking.'

'I don't care about *you*,' said Peter. 'Look what you've done! I'll probably have to pay for this out of my allowance.'

Miranda stepped on to the broken section of fence and over into the wild garden. The long, stringy grass reached up to her waist. 'At least we're in here now,' she said. She looked round at the houses on either side. 'And it doesn't look like anyone heard us, either.'

'We can prop the fence up when we come back out,' said Holly. 'No one will know the difference. I mean, come on, Peter, it would probably have fallen down all on its own, the state it's in.'

Still grumbling, Peter followed the two girls into the jungle beyond the fallen fence.

'If you have to pay for it, we'll help you out, won't we?' Holly said. 'Won't we, Miranda?'

Miranda bent down in the tall grass.

'Whoa!' she said, turning and showing them what she had picked up. 'Our ball!' she said. 'I didn't think we'd ever find it.'

Peter groaned. 'We weren't supposed to find it,' he said. 'That was the whole point.'

Miranda shrugged and tossed the ball over her shoulder. 'There,' she said. 'It's lost again. Satisfied?'

'Let's take a look at the shed,' said Holly. 'That's what we're in here for. A quick look, then we can sort the fence out. Stop looking so miserable, Peter. It'll be OK.'

With a last despairing look at the ruined fence, Peter followed Holly and Miranda as they waded through the grass towards the shed.

'Ouch!' said Miranda. 'I've been stung! It's these rotten nettles. They're everywhere.'

'You should have worn jeans like me,' said Holly.

'I don't play tennis in jeans,' said Miranda. 'Ow! Now I've scratched myself on a thorn. Oh, heck! And there are wasps! I hate wasps!' She waved her arms about. 'Shoo! Go away! Don't bite me, I taste horrible!'

'Wasps don't bite, they sting,' said Peter.

'And stop flapping about. You'll only annoy them.'

Holly reached the tumbledown shed and lifted the strut of wood away from the door. The door opened on its own on rusty hinges.

All manner of junk was piled inside. A broken old lawn-mower, paint tins, flower-pots, and heaps of other stuff, laced with cobwebs and coated with grime.

'Well?' said Peter as Holly ducked her head into the shed. 'See anything?'

'Just rubbish,' said Holly. Behind Peter, Miranda was still windmilling her arms in an effort to keep the buzzing wasps at bay. Holly stepped cautiously into the shed. It was very gloomy inside, and smelt of mould and rot.

'What are we looking for?' Peter asked from the doorway.

'Anything to show someone's been in here recently,' said Holly, wiping a trail of spider's web off her shoulder. 'This place must be spider heaven,' she said. 'Everything's covered in webs.'

Peter shuddered. 'I don't think I want to go in there,' he said. 'I'm not very fond of spiders.'

Holly grinned back at him. 'You big softie,' she said. 'Spiders can't hurt you!'

'All the same . . .' began Peter.

'Whoop!' yelled Miranda, cannoning into Peter as a particulary ferocious wasp took a dive at her.

Peter found himself in the shed whether he liked it or not. Miranda pulled the door shut behind them.

'That'll stop them,' she said. 'I think we'd better wait until they go away. I'm bound to get stung.'

With the door closed, it was almost pitch-black in the shed. The only light filtered in through cracks in the walls and roof.

'You clown!' said Holly. 'Open that door. I can't see what I'm doing.' *Crash!* Holly stumbled over something solid and fell.

'I'm not opening the door until those wasps have gone,' said Miranda.

Holly's eyes gradually adjusted to the lack of light. She'd landed on something reasonably soft. She sat up, feeling under herself.

'It feels like cardboard,' she said, running her hand along a smooth edge. She blinked a couple of times, trying to see better.

'Is it the boxes?' asked Peter, trying not to think of spiders.

'Sort of,' said Holly. 'But they're flattened out. It's a whole pile of flattened-out boxes, I think.' As she felt about in the darkness, there was a sudden burst of light from the door.

'That's better,' she said. 'I can see now.'

'What in heaven's name do you three think you're playing at?' shouted a man's voice.

Holly snapped her head round.

This was the second time they'd been caught in mid-investigation. Holly groaned. This was becoming a habit!

6 Operation car-wash

'Oh! Hello, Dad,' said Peter. 'We . . . I – you see . . .'

'Out!' ordered Mr Hamilton. He was in his office suit. There was a thunderous expression on his face as the Mystery Kids trooped sheepishly out of the shed and lined up in front of him.

'You're home early,' said Peter. 'I wasn't expecting you for another couple of hours.' He gave his father a hopeful look. 'Did you have a good day?'

'Never mind all that,' Mr Hamilton said sternly. 'What are you doing over here, and what have you done to my fence?'

'We were playing tennis,' said Holly.

'And our ball went over the fence,' continued Miranda.

'And when I tried to climb the fence,' added Holly, 'it sort of collapsed. I'm ever

60

so sorry.' She gave him a weak smile. 'We'll fix it for you.'

'You were looking for your ball?' Mr Hamilton said slowly.

'That's right,' said Peter.

'In the shed?'

'Um . . .' began Peter.

'Wasps!' said Miranda. 'We were hiding from wasps.' She looked round. The wasps had taken themselves off to another part of the garden. She pointed towards them. '*Those* wasps,' she said.

'I see,' said Mr Hamilton. Holly got the impression he wasn't entirely convinced. 'Come with me.'

They followed him back into Peter's garden.

'Peter,' he said. 'Go and fetch my toolbox.'

Peter went.

'I'm sure the fence can be mended,' said Holly.

Mr Hamilton shook his head. 'I can't leave you lot alone for five minutes, can I?' he said. '*Something* always happens when the three of you get together.'

Peter came running down the garden with his father's toolbox. It took them half an hour to get the section of fencing back in place and to hammer it home with a few well-placed nails.

, They found out why Mr Hamilton was home early. He'd taken a couple of hours off with the intention of going to the second-hand shop in Croftleigh Road and picking up a video recorder.

With the fence mended, Holly and Miranda were sent home, while Peter and his father got into their car for the trip to Square Deal to buy a video machine.

'Do you think he was annoyed?' asked Miranda as the two girls walked along together.

'Just a bit.' Holly sighed. 'I wonder if grown-up investigators have these problems?'

'What? Being caught hiding in sheds by their dads?' Miranda said with a grin. 'I doubt it. Still, it's a pity there wasn't anything interesting in there. Apart from those folded-up old boxes.'

'They weren't folded-up *old* boxes,' said Holly. 'They were folded-up new boxes.'

'What makes you say that?' asked Miranda.

'You saw the state of everything else in

that shed,' said Holly. 'If that cardboard had been there any length of time, it would have gone rotten like everything else. They must have been put in there recently.'

'Oh. Right,' said Miranda. 'So what do you make of that?'

'I don't know,' said Holly. 'But I intend to find out.'

Holly considered phoning Peter that evening, but thought better of it. She and Miranda weren't exactly Mr Hamilton's favourite people just then. It would probably be wise, she decided, to give him time to cool off.

Miranda had a late class to attend the following afternoon, so Holly met up with Peter on her own at the railway station as he got off the train home from his school.

'I'll be glad when I don't have to make that journey any more,' said Peter. 'It's been arranged for me to start at your school on Monday week.'

'Great,' said Holly. 'Our Mystery Kids work will be a lot easier with the three of us all together during the day as well as in the evenings.'

They headed off to Peter's house. Miranda

had arranged to meet them a little later, after her class.

All day, Holly had been trying to make sense of the information they had gathered.

What were the boxes for?

For putting things in.

But *what*? And *why*?

'Because they want to keep the stuff that was in the boxes secret,' said Peter as the two of them walked into his house. 'An empty house like that would be the perfect place to keep things hidden.'

'But what *sort* of things?' asked Holly.

'Guns?' Peter suggested. 'They could be international gunrunners. Or drugs?'

Holly looked unhappily at him. 'I hope it's neither of those,' she said. 'Especially not *guns*.'

'Don't worry,' said Peter. 'It won't be guns. Not in cardboard boxes. Guns would be too heavy. But I've been thinking about what you said before – about spies. Maybe the house *is* being used for surveillance. That would explain the camera.'

'And the boxes could be full of spying stuff, like I said,' added Holly. 'Do you really think so?'

'It could be private investigators,' said Peter. 'They could be watching people in another house over there. It could be a stake-out.'

'And that man who was pretending to be a meter reader is one of them,' said Holly. 'Oh! it drives me *mad*, not knowing what's going on over there!'

Peter opened his front door.

'We should write this all down when Miranda gets here,' said Peter. 'I'm sure she'll have some ideas, too.'

'I bet she will,' said Holly. 'And they'll all be to do with terrible murders.'

'Do you want to see our new video?' said Peter. He led Holly into their sitting-room. The video recorder was set up next to the television.

Peter fumbled with the controls for five minutes but the television screen stayed just a mass of white interference.

'Do you know how to work it?' asked Holly.

'Of course I do,' said Peter. 'I'm brilliant at stuff like this. Just give me a minute.'

'Where are the instructions?' asked Holly.

'I don't know,' said Peter. He nodded

across the room. 'Have a look in the box.'
A cardboard box lay open on the floor.
Holly rooted through the packaging debris,
but there was no instruction manual.

'They did *give* you an instruction leaflet,
didn't they?' asked Holly.

'Oh, I don't know,' Peter said in exasperation. 'I can't be bothered with this any more.
That's the problem with buying second-hand
stuff. Maybe there's something wrong with
it. I expect Dad will be able to figure it out.'

It wasn't long before Miranda arrived and
the Mystery Kids went up to their office to
talk things over.

'Theory number one,' said Holly, writing
in her notebook. The page was headed *Case
file: Midnight lights*. 'The house is being used
by secret agents for surveillance.'

'When did you decide that?' asked Miranda.

'We talked about it earlier,' said Peter.
'Before you got here.'

'You're not supposed to have ideas when
I'm not here,' said Miranda. 'We're supposed
to discuss these things together.'

'I can't help having ideas,' said Holly.
'What am I supposed to do? Stop thinking
when you're not around?'

'If you're putting *that* theory down,' Miranda demanded. 'Then my idea about the murderer should go down as well.'

'What? Even though it doesn't fit in with anything we've found out?' said Peter.

'What exactly *have* we found out?' said Miranda. 'For all we know, those boxes could have been full of stuff left by the previous owners.'

'So why move them in the middle of the night?' asked Peter. 'Your theory doesn't explain the flashlight from the camera, or the loose panel by the door, or that man pretending to want to read the electricity meter.'

'That's right,' said Holly. 'Those boxes are definitely the key to this whole mystery.'

'But they were *moved*,' Miranda insisted. 'They probably aren't even in the house any more.' She paused. 'Oh! Except that Sparky turned up after the boxes had been moved.'

'Which means they must still be in the house somewhere,' said Peter. 'He came back to check that everything was OK.'

'But he *couldn't* check anything because we were in there,' said Holly. 'So he'll come back again, won't he?'

'He might already have been back,' said Miranda.

'Surely it'd be worth us checking the place out again, just in case,' said Holly. The other two stared at her. She shook her head. 'I don't mean we try to get *in* there again. I mean we should come up with some plan where we can keep an eye on the house without drawing attention to ourselves. I *really* want to know what's going on in there.'

Peter sighed. 'I suppose you mean *I* should keep watch from my window.'

'No,' said Holly. 'We need to keep our eyes on the front of the house. I've had an idea.'

'Brilliant disguises?' said Miranda. 'We dress up as three privet hedges and stand in the front garden?'

'Not exactly,' said Holly. 'Car-washing!'

'Car-washing?' chorused Peter and Miranda.

Holly nodded. 'Our school has just started a fund-raising campaign for new computer terminals,' she told Peter. 'If we could get Mr Taylor to agree to us setting up a car-washing service, we could spend hours in Roseway Road without anyone suspecting anything. You never know, we might even find out who is being watched. And we'd be making money for the school. What do you say?'

Peter and Miranda looked at each other.

'Can we do it in disguise?' asked Miranda.

'No!' said Holly. 'No disguises.'

Miranda sighed. 'I never get to wear any disguises,' she said. 'What's the fun in spying on people if you can't wear disguises?'

Mr Taylor was all in favour of Holly's scheme. After a lecture on not pestering people who didn't want their cars washed, and on doing a good and thorough job, he got the school secretary to type out a letter for the three friends. The letter stated that all monies collected would be used by the school. He also gave them a form to be signed by anyone who gave them money.

They got to work on Friday afternoon. Holly attached the form to a clipboard. Armed with a bucket, a bottle of all-purpose cleaner and several sponges and cloths, they made their way into Roseway Road.

There was no answer to Holly's ring at the first three houses.

'No one's in,' she complained. 'It's too early. Perhaps we should come back later?'

'Then everyone will be eating dinner or watching their favourite TV programme,' said Peter. 'Don't give up yet.'

Holly rang at another door. A harassed-looking young woman appeared with a baby in her arms and a small child clinging to her skirt.

'Hello,' said Holly in her politest voice. She went into her prepared speech while the other two waited at the gate.

The door slammed and she walked back down the short path.

'No luck?' asked Miranda.

'No car!' said Holly.

At the next house they had more luck – or so they thought at first. The man who answered the door was delighted by their offer. Except that it wasn't a car he wanted washed. It was a huge motor-bike. It was parked on the concrete front under a grimy tarpaulin.

It was filthy. It looked as if it hadn't been used for years.

'Do a good job, mind,' said the man, after they had filled their bucket from his kitchen sink. 'I'm not paying up until it's spotless.'

It took the three of them over an hour to clean the motor-bike to his satisfaction. He even had them polishing the metalwork and rubbing at the leather seat until they could almost see their faces in it.

They did their best to keep an eye on the empty house.

'Look at me!' said Miranda as they collected their money and came back out on to the pavement. 'I'm absolutely filthy! I'm fed up with this. And there hasn't been a sign of anyone going *near* that house. I'm going home!'

'Miranda!' called Holly as her friend marched off down the road. 'Don't give up!'

'Too late,' Miranda yelled back. 'I quit!'

Peter looked unhappily at Holly.

'It's OK,' she said. 'She'll come back once she's calmed down.'

But Miranda didn't come back. Peter and Holly cleaned three cars before they gave up as well. It really was beginning to look as if they were wasting their time.

'Oh, well,' Holly said eventually. 'At least we made a bit of money for the school.

Tomorrow's Saturday. I'll give Miranda a call in the morning and we can have another meeting. Perhaps we'll be able to come up with another idea by then.'

The car-washing plan had proved to be a lot of hard work for nothing.

Boxes in, boxes out

Holly had only just got out of bed on Saturday morning when Miranda appeared at the front door, dressed in an old T-shirt and torn jeans.

'Well?' she said. 'Are we washing cars today or not?'

'I thought you were sick of it,' said Holly.

'Yesterday I was. Today I'm not,' said Miranda. 'Today I'm full of enthusiasm.'

Holly looked suspiciously at her. 'Why?'

Miranda grinned. 'Mum's decided our house needs spring-cleaning,' she said. 'This was the only way I could get out of it.'

'It isn't spring,' said Holly.

Miranda laughed. 'Try telling that to my mum,' she said. 'Come on, slowcoach, let's go and root Peter out. I've got a feeling we're going to be lucky today.'

73

Peter was as surprised as Holly by Miranda's change of heart, until he learned the reason.

'Is washing cars easier than spring-cleaning, then?' he asked as they walked down to Roseway Road with their equipment.

'It is when Mum's gone out and left Becky and Rachel in charge,' said Miranda. Becky and Rachel were Miranda's older twin sisters. 'I'd rather slave for us than slave for them,' said Miranda.

They had much better luck this time. There were plenty of people in, and once they'd been told the money would be going to the local school, most people were more than happy to have the three friends wash their cars.

Holly's bum-bag was getting quite heavy with coins by lunch-time. The only disappointment was that in the three hours they'd been working, no one had gone into the empty house.

At midday they had a brief rest, sitting on a wall across the road from the house and a little way down the street. Peter handed chocolate bars round.

'If no one goes there today, do we have to come back tomorrow?' asked Miranda.

'We'll run out of cars to clean by then,' said Peter. 'In fact, if something doesn't happen pretty soon, we're going to be so far down the road we won't even be able to see the house any more.'

'Something will happen,' said Holly.

'Ha!' Miranda mumbled through a chunk of chocolate.

All three of them were wet and grubby from their work. Half a bucket of soapy water had gone all over Miranda's shoes and it was only the thought of being ordered about by her sisters that stopped her from squelching off home. Holly's arms were aching so much she hardly had the strength to wring out the cleaning cloth.

They were just about to ring at yet another door when a small van came cruising past. *Drip-Busters!* proclaimed the sign on the side. *Twenty-four-hour plumbers.*

The van came to a stop at the kerb outside the empty house and two men got out.

'Look!' squealed Miranda.

'Don't *watch* them,' said Holly. 'Pretend we're busy.'

The three of them went back to polishing the last car they had been working on.

Something was finally happening!

The men were in overalls. One of them went round to open the back doors of the van, whilst the other headed up the path to the empty house's front door.

The man at the back of the van was wearing a baseball cap low over his eyes.

Holly tried to see what the other man was doing in the sunken doorway, but the trailing jasmine was in the way. When he came back down the path, she could see that the front door had been opened.

'Did you see him at that loose bit of glass?' hissed Peter. 'Was that how he got the door open, or did he have a key?'

'I couldn't see,' said Holly, peering over the bonnet of the car.

As the three friends watched, the men began ferrying boxes into the house.

'See the short one with the baseball cap?' said Peter. 'I've seen him somewhere before.'

'Keep down!' said Holly. 'Don't stare at them. Miranda, look *busy*, will you? Don't let them see we're watching them.'

'I wish that cap wasn't shading his face so much,' said Peter. 'If I can just get one good look at him, I'm sure I'll remember where

I've seen him before.'

For the next few minutes the two men busied themselves with carrying boxes into the house.

'If they're the people doing the surveillance,' said Miranda, crouching down and rubbing at a hub-cap while she peeped round the front bumper of the car, 'how come they're taking more stuff *in* there?'

'Maybe this is a whole new lot of surveillance gear,' said Peter. 'I bet that's what it is. They're probably bringing in even more sophisticated stuff.'

'I'd love to know for certain what's going on in there,' said Holly.

One of the men came out of the house and closed the back of the van before disappearing inside again.

Several minutes went past with no further sign of the men.

Holly stood up. 'What do you think they're doing in there?'

'Setting up their equipment,' said Peter. 'Holly, write down the number plate of the van. If we're going to find out who these people are, we need all the information we can get.'

'I've already done it,' said Holly. She showed Peter the clipboard. She had written down the details of the van, and a brief description of the two men. 'I don't need you telling me how to collect evidence,' she said. 'I've even got the time they arrived.'

'I'm going over there for a quick look,' said Miranda.

'Don't be daft,' said Holly. 'They're bound to come out and catch you.'

'So?' said Miranda. 'I'll ask them if they want their van cleaned. They're not going to know we're watching them. We want to try and find out who they are, don't we?'

Miranda walked across the road, her wet trainers squelching.

'Oh, no! Just listen to her!' Holly groaned as Miranda started whistling innocently. 'She always does that when she's trying to be cunning.'

At the van, Miranda turned and gave a quick thumbs-up sign and grinned at them.

She walked up the path of the empty house. The door was open a couple of centimetres, but the glass panel was in its proper place. If the men had got in that way, they had covered their tracks well.

She reached towards the door. She had her speech all ready.

She hesitated as she saw the blurry shape of a man in the hall through the glass door-panels.

'One half now, the rest later,' she heard a man say.

The door opened from the inside.

The two men were in the hall, weighed down by boxes.

'Oh, hello,' said Miranda. 'I just wondered if you'd like us to wash your van. We're—'

'No, we don't,' snapped the man at the door. He was a big man, with short greying hair and a face like a bulldog.

Miranda looked for any sign of nervousness or alarm on the men's faces. Anything that would give her some proof that they were up to something secretive. But there was nothing, apart from the fact that they were both a bit sweaty and red-faced from their work.

'It's for a good cause,' said Miranda.

'We don't need our van cleaned,' said the big man, stepping forwards so that Miranda was forced to back down the path, the hanging jasmine catching in her hair as she did so.

'Our school's collecting for new computer stuff,' Miranda said as she backed out on to the pavement.

The man looked over his shoulder. 'Gary,' he said, 'give the kid some money.'

Across the road, Holly and Peter were watching with bated breath. What did Miranda think she was doing?

The man put the box down on the pavement and opened the back doors of the van. Miranda hovered nearby while the two men loaded their boxes into the van.

'Here,' said the man called Gary. He put his hand in his overall pocket and took out some coins.

'Oh, we can't take it for *nothing*,' said Miranda. 'We'd have to do something in exchange. If you don't want your van cleaned, maybe we could help you loading stuff?'

The big man gave her an angry frown. He grabbed her wrist, scooped the coins out of Gary's hand and put them in hers. 'Take the money,' he said. 'Take it and go and bother someone else. We're busy.'

'If you're *sure*,' said Miranda.

'I'm sure,' said the big man. 'Scram!'

'OK,' said Miranda. 'Thanks a lot.'

She ran over to where Holly and Peter were waiting.

'You nutcase,' hissed Peter. 'What was all that about?'

'I was trying to see what they had in those boxes,' whispered Miranda.

'And?' asked Holly.

Miranda shook her head. 'I couldn't see anything,' she said. 'But they gave me some money.' She opened her fist and showed them the coins. 'They just wanted to get rid of me.' She told them what she had heard the big man say. '"One half now, the rest later."'

'They're looking over here,' whispered Holly. 'We'd better look as if we're doing something.'

They went to another house and rang the bell, doing their best not to look as if they were watching the two men.

The man who answered the door agreed to pay them to wash his car. Peter went through to fill their bucket while the girls waited on the path.

'The one in the baseball cap is called Gary,'

Miranda told Holly. 'And if we want a code-name for the other one, I think we should call him Bruiser. He looks like a real thug.'

Holly nodded and wrote the two names down.

Over the next few minutes the two men ferried boxes out of the empty house and stacked them in the back of the van.

'I don't get it,' said Miranda. 'Why did they take boxes in and then bring them straight out again?' A slosh of soapy water splashed down Miranda's jeans. 'Peter! Be careful, I'm wet enough as it is!'

The men got into the cab of the van and drove off. As the van rumbled away the three friends stopped their work and looked at one another.

'Maybe they weren't the same boxes,' said Peter.

Holly shook her head. 'Didn't you notice anything odd?' she said. 'Didn't you notice that the boxes seemed a lot lighter when they took them in than when they brought them out?'

'That's right,' said Peter. 'They carried a couple of boxes each on the way in, but only one on the way out.'

'Whoo!' breathed Miranda. 'Empty boxes *in* and full boxes *out*! Holly, you're right. They weren't putting stuff in the house. They were taking stuff out!'

Stolen goods

'Are you washing that car, or just standing and looking at it?' The man whose car they were supposed to be cleaning was on his doorstep, hands on hips, frowning at them.

They got back to work.

A few minutes later, and with a couple more coins in Holly's bag, the Mystery Kids gathered on the corner of Roseway Road to decide what they should do next.

'Did you get a good look at the man in the baseball cap?' Peter asked Miranda. 'Did you recognise him?'

'What, Gary?' said Miranda. She shook her head.

'He wasn't the fake meter reader, then?' said Holly.

'No,' said Miranda. 'I've never seen that Gary man before in my life.'

'Well, *I* have,' insisted Peter. 'I just wish I could remember where.'

'What do we do now?' asked Miranda.

'The big man said they were taking half now and the rest later, didn't he?' said Holly. 'Which means that whatever they were up to, they're clearing out, right?'

'It looks like it,' said Peter. 'Rats! Now we'll never know!'

'But there's still stuff in the house,' said Holly.

'Hold on a minute,' said Peter. 'If you're thinking what I *think* you're thinking, you can forget it.'

Miranda looked bemused. 'What do you think she's thinking?'

'I think she's thinking about going back in that house,' said Peter.

'It's our last chance of finding out what's been going on in there,' said Holly.

'Now look here,' said Miranda. 'We tried the front and got caught. We tried the *back* and got caught. What next? Tunnelling up from underneath, or are you planning on us parachuting down the chimney out of an aeroplane?'

'In through the front again,' said Holly.

'That's the easiest way. And this time we go straight upstairs. *That's* where Peter saw the lights, so that's where the rest of the stuff will be. It won't take us more than two minutes.'

'But Bruiser said they were coming back for the rest,' said Miranda. 'They'll catch us.'

'They will if we stand here arguing about it all afternoon,' said Holly. 'Look, they've only been gone ten minutes. They've got to get to wherever they're going, unload the stuff and get back again. We've got plenty of time.'

'Do you think they're up to something illegal?' asked Miranda.

'It's certainly something they don't want anyone to know about,' said Peter. 'I'm with Holly. This is our only chance to find out.'

'If we get caught,' said Miranda, '*you* can think up your own excuses, right? I'm going to plead insanity.'

Peter laughed. 'We'll back you up on *that* one,' he said.

Holly didn't say anything to her friends, but her stomach was turning over anxiously as the three of them walked back to the house. But she knew that if they didn't act *now* then they would *never* solve the mystery. And an unsolved mystery would nag at her for the rest of her *life!*

She glanced round. The street was empty.

'OK,' she said firmly. 'Here goes.'

They bundled into the doorway. It took only a moment to edge the glass panel open and reach in to turn the lock.

Once inside, they closed the door and replaced the panel.

Miranda shivered. 'This is a really bad idea,' she mumbled. 'We're going to get caught. I know we are.'

'No, we aren't,' said Holly. 'Trust me.'

Miranda gave a hollow laugh.

'Come on,' said Peter. 'We haven't got time to argue about it now.'

Holly led the way upstairs. The bare stair treads creaked under their feet. Miranda's groan of unease echoed eerily in the stairwell. The stairs went up to a long landing with four doors leading off it. All four doors were closed.

Holly opened the first door. The room was quite bare. Peter pushed the second door open and they found themselves looking into a bathroom.

They tiptoed along the landing and Holly opened another door into an empty room. They looked at one another. There was only one door left now. Only one more room. Holly wondered whether her frantic heart-beats sounded as loud to the others as they did to her. *Thump-thump, thump-thump.*

She turned the handle and pushed the door open.

Peter let out a groan of exasperation.

There was nothing in the room.

'Well?' said Miranda. 'Now what?'

'The stuff must be downstairs,' said Peter. 'We should have checked the ground floor first.'

'Now he tells us,' said Miranda. She looked along the landing, as if hoping a fifth door might suddenly have appeared.

'Hey,' she said, glancing upwards. 'Look!' A square opening was set into the ceiling above their heads.

'That just leads up into the roof space,' said Peter. 'You'd need a ladder to get up there.'

'So let's look for a ladder,' said Holly.

'Don't be daft,' said Peter. 'If those men had the stuff up there, the ladder would be here, wouldn't it?' He headed for the stairs. 'I'm going to look downstairs.'

'Wait!' said Miranda.

'Come on,' Peter said as he ran down the stairs. 'We're running out of time.'

'Coming?' Holly asked Miranda. Every second that passed was making her more uneasy. She wanted to get out of the house as quickly as possible, whether they found anything or not.

'Just hold on a second,' said Miranda. She had spotted something. A long pole resting in the corner. A pole with a metal hook on the end. She picked it up and looked again at the trap-door in the ceiling.

'Got it!' she said. 'See that ring?' Holly looked. There was a metal ring at one side of the trap-door. 'This hook goes into the ring so you can push the thing open,' said Miranda. 'Watch.'

It took her a couple of attempts before she got the long pole under control and managed to slip the hook into the ring. She gave a hefty shove. The trap-door didn't move.

'Oh!' she said. 'I was *sure*—'

'Don't push it,' said Holly. 'Pull it. Why are you always so useless with things like

that? It opens downwards.' She took hold
of the pole alongside Miranda and they both
gave a good hard tug. The trap-door grated
open and the feet of a metal ladder slid out
of the gap.

'Wow!' gasped Miranda. 'A ladder! Come
on, Holly. Pull!'

They forced the trap-door wider and the
ladder edged down through the hole.

'There must be some kind of machinery up
there,' said Holly. 'Attached to the door, so
the ladder slides out when you open it. Give
me the pole. It must pull right down.'

'I can do it,' said Miranda.

'Don't argue,' said Holly, trying to get the
pole out of Miranda's hands. 'You'll do it all
wrong.'

'Get off!' said Miranda. 'I found it!' She
elbowed Holly out of the way.

'Miranda!' exclaimed Holly. 'Don't be so
childish!' She made another lunge for the
pole. 'We can do it together.'

But the hook on the end of the pole was
still caught in the ring. The two of them
fought to get it free. There was a sudden,
sharp noise and the pole came free.

'Oh, brilliant!' said Miranda. 'Now look

what you've done!' The hook had come off the end of the pole and was dangling uselessly in the ring.

'Don't blame me,' said Holly. 'You were the one fighting to do it by yourself. I said you'd mess it up, didn't I?'

With a snort of annoyance, Miranda yanked the pole out of Holly's hands and made a few attempts to jerk the ladder down.

'You'll never do it like that,' said Holly. She jumped up at the legs of the ladder. Her fingertips just scraped the foot. It was just out of reach.

'Peter's taller than us,' said Miranda. 'He'll be able to reach it.'

'Wait,' said Holly. 'If you support me, I can climb up on the banister rail.' The banister ran the length of the landing, preventing a fall into the stairwell.

'Are you sure?' asked Miranda.

'Of course I'm sure,' said Holly. 'But hurry!'

Miranda made her hands into a stirrup. Holly took a firm grip of Miranda's shoulder and lifted herself. She got one foot on top of the banister rail, her hand pressing down on Miranda's head as she boosted herself into the air. Miranda sagged under the weight.

For a second Holly teetered perilously in the air, trying to find her balance. She grabbed at the ladder and it came screeching down with the teeth-grating sound of metal on metal.

The two girls tumbled to the floor as the ladder thudded down beside them.

'Ha!' Holly laughed, springing to her feet. 'Got it!'

Miranda sat up. 'You never do anything the easy way, do you?' she said.

Holly took no notice. She climbed the ladder.

Miranda stood up and held the bottom of the ladder as she saw her friend's upper half disappear into the dark hole.

'Well?' she called up. 'Anything?'

'Wow!'

'What?' Miranda climbed the ladder. '*What?*'

Holly clambered into the roof space. It was dark in there, but enough light filtered in through a filthy skylight for her to see. And what she saw, as she crouched on the floor up there, brought another 'Wow!' from her.

'What have you found?' asked Miranda. Her head came up into the roof space. 'Wow!' she breathed. 'Aladdin's Cave!'

It hadn't taken Peter more than a few seconds to check the ground-floor rooms. He checked the front room that Holly had seen through the bay window the other day and the back room with the French windows where they had first seen the boxes. Both were empty.

He ran down the three steps into the back kitchen. There was an old sink unit under a window and a couple of empty cupboards. But still no sign of any cardboard boxes.

It didn't make sense. Miranda had said she'd heard one of the men say they were coming back for the rest of their stuff. But where *was* the rest?

Had Miranda not heard correctly? Had the men decided to take everything in one go after all? Where *was* it?

He came out of the kitchen, baffled and frustrated. A door faced him. He hadn't spotted it on his way into the kitchen. A door under the stairs. It might just be a cupboard. On the other hand . . .

He opened the door. Steps led down into darkness. It was a cellar.

Peter grinned. That had to be it! Of course! The stuff would have been put somewhere safe. It wouldn't just be left lying around for anyone to find.

He pushed the door back against the wall. He tried the light switch, shaking his head at his own stupidity as the light failed to come on.

The electricity would have been turned off ages ago. He already *knew* that, but at least the girls weren't there to make fun of his silly action.

I'll just have to risk it in the dark, he thought.

He paused, every sense terribly alert as he heard a sound from the front of the house. The ominous sound of a large vehicle drawing up at the kerb.

Peter ran to the front door, his heart in his mouth, and peered through the glass.

The van was back.

9 Hide and seek

Even as Peter ducked down out of sight, two men were getting out of the cab of the van. The big man was there, but he didn't have Gary with him this time. The other man with him was Sparky. Peter recognised him immediately. So the fake meter reader *was* involved.

Peter hesitated long enough to see them go round to the back of the van and open the doors.

He ran to the foot of the stairs.

'Holly!' He tried to project his voice up the stairs in a frantic whisper. 'Miranda! They're *back*! Quick!'

There was no answer. All he heard was a loud, metallic grating noise and a heavy thud. What were they *doing* up there?

He glanced round at the door. Through the frosted glass he could see the blurry shapes of the men coming up the path. There was no time for the girls to get down here even if they had heard him. They'd be caught on the stairs. And *then* what would happen?

Peter's brain raced. There was nothing upstairs – they'd already made sure of that. Holly and Miranda were bound to hear the men come into the house. If they had any sense, they'd keep quiet as mice up there and wait until the men finished what they were doing and went away again.

Or would they? Peter hesitated for a moment, then went haring up the stairs to warn the two girls.

'Look at all this!' said Holly. Dust drifted in the air up into the roof space. The bare floor beams had been covered with plywood, and heaped all around the trap-door was a curious collection of things. There were video recorders and dismantled hi-fi units and cameras. There were piles of compact discs and handbags and wallets and jewellery boxes. There were silver ornaments and clocks. It was as if all the valuables from a dozen or more houses had been stashed away up here. There were even a couple of small portable televisions, trailing their wires across the floor.

Miranda had been right – it *was* like Aladdin's Cave up here. A criminal Aladdin's Cave.

'This isn't surveillance stuff,' said Holly. 'It looks like *stolen* stuff.' She stared at Miranda. 'They aren't using this place for *watching* anything – they're using it to stash stolen things.'

'The burglaries!' Miranda gasped. 'Remember that man from next door said there had been a lot of burglaries in the area? Holly – what on earth have we got ourselves into?'

'We've got to call the police,' said Holly. 'Quickly! Before they come back.'

Miranda pulled a tissue out of her pocket and held it to her face, trying to keep the dust from making her sneeze.

'They must have been burgling away like maniacs to get all this lot!' said Holly. 'There must be a *fortune* up here.'

'Don't just sit there looking at it,' said Miranda. 'We've got to get out of here.'

'Hoy!' It was a sharp hiss from beneath them. Miranda looked down and saw Peter's frightened face. 'They're *back*!'

'They're criminals!' said Miranda. 'The attic is full of stolen stuff!'

'*What?*' Peter gasped in horror.

'They're burglars!' called Holly.

'Get down out of there,' panted Peter. 'We've got to hide.'

'Right,' said Holly. 'I'm coming. Out of the way.'

She crawled to the trap-door. Miranda climbed down the ladder. As her foot touched the floor she heard the front door open beneath her.

'Get a move on!' she whispered up to Holly.

Holly's frightened face stared down at her through the hole. 'Hide! I'm coming.'

Peter grabbed Miranda's arm.

'In here,' he said, dragging her towards the bathroom door. 'Holly, quick!'

As Peter hauled her through the bathroom door, Miranda glanced back. She could see Holly's foot coming down through the hole. Would she get down in time?

In her panic to get out of the roof space, Holly caught her jeans on the top of the ladder. She tugged wildly, trying to free herself, but a sharp edge of the ladder had snagged right through her jeans leg. The more she struggled to free herself, the worse it got.

With a soft yelp of despair, she lifted herself back up into the roof space. Above the hammering of her heart, she could hear the voices of the men coming up the stairs.

Over to one side, where the slope of the roof met the plywood flooring, was a thick roll of something. Not carpet – some kind of thick insulation material. Holly scampered over to it and stretched herself out behind it.

She forced herself to lie perfectly still. As long as the men didn't actually look over there, she had a chance of remaining hidden until they went away.

As she lay there listening to the throbbing of her heart, she hoped that Miranda and Peter had managed to get themselves hidden away safely.

Holly Adams, she thought to herself, *you are the stupidest person in the entire world! You and your mysteries! Look at the mess you're in now!*

Miranda and Peter crouched behind the bathroom door, straining to hear. Miranda spotted the catch by the handle and silently slid it closed.

'Come on,' she heard one of the men say. 'We haven't got all day.' She recognised the voice. It was Bruiser.

'I thought I heard something,' came another man's voice from further away.

'Mice,' said Bruiser. 'Get up here.' He was on the landing now, horribly close to the door behind which Miranda was crouching in terror.

'That fool,' she heard Bruiser say. 'I told Gary to put the ladder up.' He had obviously seen that the trap-door was open and that the ladder was down. 'He's going to get us all caught. What if that estate agent woman had brought someone here? I should wring his neck!'

That would be handy, thought Miranda. *That would be one less burglar to deal with, at least.* She gave Peter an anxious look. Peter looked as scared as she felt.

'You know what he's like,' said the second man, his voice much closer now. Miranda recognised Sparky's voice.

'Yes,' snarled Bruiser. 'Useless!'

'Forget it,' said Sparky. 'No one's been

here, and we'll have all the stuff out of here in ten minutes. You worry too much.'

'We're going to need some more boxes,' said Bruiser. Peter and Miranda heard the metallic creak of the ladder as he stepped on the first rung. 'Where did Gary put them?'

'In the shed out back,' said Sparky.

'What? Why?' Bruiser sounded exasperated. 'Why did he put them out there?'

'You told him to hide them,' said Sparky. 'And they wouldn't go through the trapdoor. Do you want me to go and fetch them?'

'No. Leave it. We'll see how we get on with what we've got,' said Bruiser. 'We don't want to risk being seen in the garden unless we have to. Gary's a bigger idiot than you. I should have just strangled him then and there the other night when he set off that camera! I'm surrounded by fools!' The ladder creaked as he climbed. 'I'm going to beat Gary's brains out when we get back to the shop,' he said. 'I knew we couldn't rely on him.'

They heard Sparky laugh. 'What brains?' he said.

That explains the flash of light, thought

Peter. *One of them set a flashbulb off by accident.*

Bruiser said something that they didn't catch. Judging by the tone of his voice, Miranda felt quite glad she hadn't heard properly. It didn't sound particularly polite.

Bruiser's voice echoed from further away. *He must be up in the roof space now.* Miranda looked at Peter and crossed her fingers. He nodded. Their only hope was that Holly was well hidden up there. All this talk of necks being wrung and brains being beaten out was very alarming.

Holly held her breath, trying to flatten herself against the floor. Trying to make herself as small as possible behind the roll of material.

Please don't look this way, she prayed.

She heard a man scrabbling about only a few metres from where she was hiding.

'Ready?' she heard him call down.

A second voice drifted up. 'Yes. Start handing it down.'

There were grunts and scrapings as the man lowered things down for his partner on the ladder to take.

'Shall I fill the boxes as we go?' called the second man.

'No, let's get it all down out of here first.'

It seemed like a lifetime to Holly as she listened to the two men heaving the stolen stuff down from the attic. But at least there was one crumb of comfort – Miranda and Peter hadn't been discovered. Maybe they would be able to get out of the house and phone the police.

'OK,' said the first man. 'Just the small stuff now.'

'Are we taking the jewellery and stuff to Gary's place?' asked the second man.

'Don't be stupid,' said the first man. 'Gary just gets the electrical stuff. All the rest is going off to a man I know. He'll give us cash.'

She heard a final grunt and groan from the man. 'That's the lot,' he said. 'Gah! My back!'

'You're getting old!' laughed the second man.

'Watch it! I'm not too old to teach you a lesson or two. I'll just—' The man's voice came to an abrupt halt. Holly heard the hiss of his breath. *Clump! Clump! Clump!* In three long strides the man covered the gap between the trap-door and Holly's hiding-place.

Holly let out a stifled yell as a rough hand grabbed her collar and she was dragged out into the open.

'What is it?' yelled the other man.

Blazingly angry eyes bored into Holly as she struggled hopelessly in the man's powerful grip.

'Get up here,' he yelled. He gave Holly a ferocious shake. 'We've got trouble!'

10 Trouble with a capital T

Miranda and Peter could hear every word the men spoke from their hiding-place behind the bathroom door. They heard Bruiser call down, 'That's the lot.'

Peter grabbed Miranda's arm, making her jump.

He put his mouth close to her ear.

'We're OK,' he whispered. 'They haven't found her.'

Miranda nodded. A few minutes more and the men would leave the house. They'd be safe!

She uncrossed her fingers and let out a sigh of relief. The sigh turned into a gasp of misery as the man on the landing yelled suddenly and she heard scuffling noises from above her.

Peter's fingers dug into her arm.

There was no doubt about what had

happened up there. Holly had been caught!

'We've got to help her,' whispered Peter.

'How?' breathed Miranda. What could they do? If they were discovered, it wouldn't take those men ten seconds to overpower them. And then what might happen? Miranda didn't even want to think about it.

Peter stared round the room. There was a pedestal basin, a bath, a toilet and a small wall cupboard. There was nothing in there that they could possibly use to try and rescue Holly.

But there was a way for them to escape. A small frosted-glass window above the toilet cistern.

Miranda pointed to it.

Peter nodded, bringing his mouth close to her ear again. 'You get out,' he whispered. 'Call the police.'

'What about you?' said Miranda.

'I'll think of something,' said Peter. 'I'll try and delay them.'

Miranda crept across the floor. She climbed on to the toilet cistern, jerking at the handle of the window. It was stiff, but panic lent her strength, and, after a few hefty yanks, the handle turned and she was able to shove the window open.

She looked round at Peter. He was standing by the door, his face white.

'Good luck,' he mouthed at her. 'Be *careful*!'

She leaned out of the window, forcing her shoulders into the narrow gap. The side wall fell a clear four metres down to the garden. Too far to jump, even if she could get herself feet first through the window.

But a thick black pipe was anchored to the wall only a few centimetres to the right of the window. If she could somehow haul herself out of the window, maybe she could shin down the pipe.

Using every ounce of her strength, Miranda edged herself out through the window, twisting to catch hold of the pipe. She swivelled her hips, sat on the narrow sill and tried to draw her legs up to give herself some base from which she could swing out on to the pipe.

Her swinging foot caught on the flushing lever at the side of the cistern and she almost fell head first as the lever gave way beneath her. There was a rush of water as the toilet flushed.

She gathered herself together, and, silently

praying that the pipe would hold, brought her feet up under her on the sill and swung out into empty air.

'Let go of me!' shouted Holly, twisting in Bruiser's grip, her legs kicking as he held her in the air. 'Let me *go*!'

He released her and she crashed to the floor.

She sat up, winded but unhurt. The powerful man stood over her. The head and shoulders of the second man – Sparky – appeared through the trap-door.

'It's one of those kids!' he gasped, his eyes round with amazement. 'They were in here a few days ago. With that estate agent woman.'

'Is that a fact?' growled Bruiser. 'And they were hanging about outside earlier as well.' He crouched over Holly, his angry face only centimetres from hers. 'Where are the others?'

'What others?' said Holly.

He caught hold of her shoulder and shook her roughly.

'Don't play games with me,' he snarled. 'There were three of you. The big-mouthed blonde girl and that weasel-faced boy. Where are they?' His eyes swivelled round the roof space, looking for the others. His eyes fixed on a huge water tank. 'Aha!'

'They're not here,' said Holly.

'Is that so?' said Bruiser. He let go of her and pounced towards the tank. 'I've got you!' he shouted. 'Come on out!' He gave a growl of annoyance as he saw that there was no one hidden there.

'What are we going to do?' shouted Sparky.

The big man came back to where Holly was sitting.

'Get up,' he said.

Holly scrambled to her feet, hoping that her shaking legs wouldn't collapse under her. She was determined not to show just how frightened she was.

'My friends aren't here,' she said steadily. 'They went to call the police. They'll be here any moment.'

Sparky gave a yell and vanished.

'Wait!' bellowed Bruiser.

'I'm getting out of here,' came Sparky's voice from below them. 'I'm not hanging around to be caught!'

'Idiot!' shouted Bruiser. 'They haven't called

the police. She wouldn't be up here if they'd called the police. The other kids are in this house somewhere. Find them!'

'You find them!' Sparky yelled from the landing.

'Stop where you are!' shouted Bruiser. 'I'm coming down.' She pushed Holly ahead of him. She climbed down the ladder. Sparky was standing at the head of the stairs. Holly thought that he looked even more scared than her.

Bruiser descended, his hand locking on Holly's shoulder again as he glared at Sparky.

'Search every room,' he said. 'Get those kids!'

'But the *police*,' moaned Sparky.

'Shut up about the police,' said Bruiser. 'Are you thick, or what? She wouldn't have been hiding up there if they'd called the police. They're just nosing around on the off-chance.'

'Oh, yes?' exclaimed Holly. 'So how come we know what you've been up to? We've been watching this place for days. We know *everything*.'

The big man's grip was like a vice on her shoulder. 'Is that a fact?' he growled. He

110

looked at his accomplice. 'Don't just stand there! Search!'

Sparky hesitated for a moment, as if torn between bolting down the stairs and obeying the big man. Then he ran to the first room, sending the door crashing open.

He ran out again and hurled himself at the second door.

Holly held her breath as Sparky twisted the handle on the bathroom door and crashed face first against it as it failed to open. Miranda and Peter had locked it from inside, Holly realised. But how long would the door stay closed against two strong men?

Sparky reeled back, clutching his nose and howling. He'd hit that door with plenty of force.

'Kick it in!' shouted Bruiser.

'I've busted my nose!' yelled Sparky.

'You clown,' growled Bruiser. 'Hold her! I'll do it!'

As the big man braced himself to give the locked bathroom door a shoulder-charge, the most unexpected sound in the world came from the room beyond.

The distinct sound of a toilet flushing.

'Stop!' It was Peter's voice from beyond

the door, shouting frantically. 'I'm coming out!'

Bruiser gave Holly a nasty smile. 'So they've gone for the police, have they?' he said. He rattled the door handle and hammered on the door. 'Get out here,' he shouted.

'I'm trying,' came Peter's voice from within the bathroom. 'The lock's stuck.'

Bruiser growled. Holly could tell from his expression that he wasn't just going to stand around waiting while Peter fiddled with the lock.

Holly's mind raced. Sparky was holding her by one arm, and she could feel that he was shaking. She was certain that the lock wasn't really stuck. This was her best chance to escape, while the big man was being distracted by Peter.

Bruiser backed away from the door and charged with one hefty shoulder lowered. The door opened a split second before he hit it, catching him off-balance. Holly heard a cry from Peter as the door crashed open and the big man went careering into the room.

Holly gulped in a huge breath and let out a piercing scream. Sparky jumped with surprise, his fingers loosening on her arm as she twisted herself free and leaped for the stairs.

Peter was almost knocked off his feet as the door came smashing open under Bruiser's charge. The big man staggered, falling as he burst into the room, his hands grabbing for Peter.

But Peter was too quick for him. He ran out into the hallway just as Holly let out her scream and got free of Sparky.

'Run!' he yelled to Holly. But Holly was already ahead of him, bounding down the stairs.

Peter leaped after her, but was brought to a halt as a hand grabbed his collar and tipped him over backwards on the stairs.

It had taken Sparky only a moment to recover from the shock of Holly's escape. He pulled Peter down and dived towards Holly, his fingers clawing at her fleeing back.

Holly let out a cry as she felt a jerk on her hair.

'Got you!' yelled Sparky.

Holly was almost at the foot of the stairs. Clinging on to the banister rail, she twisted her head, trying to pull free.

Holly didn't see exactly what happened next, but Peter did. As he pulled himself to his feet, he saw Sparky trip on the stairs and fall forwards past Holly and into the hallway.

Then Bruiser came blundering out of the bathroom and Peter leaped down the stairs. Sparky was just getting to his feet – and now he was between them and the front door.

'This way!' Holly yelled, spinning round the banister rail. With Sparky between them and the front of the house, their only hope of escape was out through the back.

Peter raced after Holly as she headed alongside the stairs.

They dashed into the kitchen and Holly struggled briefly with the handle of the back door. But it wouldn't budge.

Bruiser's feet thundered on the stairs, and as Holly and Peter looked round, they saw Sparky at the kitchen door, his face twisted with anger.

'Peter! The window!' yelled Holly.

Peter's head snapped round. The window was over the sink unit. He jumped up on to the top of the unit and grabbed for the handle. It wasn't locked, but he wasn't prepared for how easily the window sprang open. With a cry, he fell head first through the window and landed, sprawling, in the garden.

Holly was only a second behind him. She heard Sparky give a yell and saw him spring towards her out of the corner of her eye. She hurled herself on to the sink unit, but Sparky was too quick for her. A hand closed round her ankle and jerked her backwards.

She struggled, feeling the unit come away from the wall. The sink unit wasn't built to withstand this sort of pressure. The water pipes ruptured and sent a blast of water into Sparky's face. For a split second, he floundered against the powerful gush of water. Then he fell.

The water fountained into the air from the broken pipe. Holly also crashed to the ground, her feet sliding on the flooded floor.

Sparky lay quite still as the water swirled round him. But even as Holly scrambled to her feet, Bruiser came bursting into the room. He took one look at the chaos and let out a bellow of rage.

Holly dived for the open window. But

she was too late. A strong arm caught her and dragged her backwards out into the hallway.

'You're coming with me,' Bruiser snarled as he half-carried her along the hallway towards the front door. 'No one's going to try and stop me while I've got you as a hostage!'

Holly in trouble

As Miranda edged her way down the pipe, she heard a crash from within the room. The men had broken in – Peter was caught! She lost her grip and fell with a brief scream down to the ground.

She fell about two metres into an overgrown flower-bed that lay against the wall. Feathery seeds billowed up around her as she scrambled to her feet. She had landed well, but as she made a dash for safety, one of her feet caught on some hidden wire and she was sent sprawling on her face.

For a few agonising seconds she tried to untangle her shoe from the clutching wire. With a scream of frustration, she kicked the shoe off and staggered to her feet. The garden fence was only six metres away. Once over that she would be in Peter's garden, and only a sprint away from the telephone. *If* she made it. And if she could get *into* Peter's house!

She ploughed through the tall grass.

'What in heaven's name is going on over there?' she heard.

She spun round. A familiar old face stared at her over the side fence. An angry face under a floppy old fishing-hat. It was Mr Frazer, the bad-tempered next-door neighbour.

'You again!' he shouted. 'I might have known!'

'Help!' yelled Miranda. 'Burglars! My friends! In there!' She was out of breath and frantic with panic. It was hardly surprising that she didn't make much sense as she blundered through the grass towards the side fence.

'Help?' shouted the old man. 'I'll give you *help*! I'm going to call the police this time. *That*'s what I'm going to do!'

'Good!' yelled Miranda. 'Do it! Do it *now*!'

She hardly knew where she got the strength from. As the astonished old man backed away, she made a flying leap over the fence and landed in his garden.

'Phone the police!' Miranda screamed. 'Quick! Before they get away!'

Mr Frazer stared at her in disbelief as she rushed past him towards the house.

'Now, look here,' he shouted, chasing her in through the open back door.

An old woman sat at the kitchen table, peeling potatoes.

'Where's your phone?' yelled Miranda. 'Quickly, please! I've got to call the police!'

'It's in the hall,' said the woman. 'But—'

'Thanks.'

Mr Frazer came to a halt in the hall as he heard Miranda gabbling into the telephone.

'What's going on?' he puffed. 'Will you please explain—'

Miranda slammed the phone down. 'No time,' she panted. 'I've got to get back.'

She almost knocked Mr Frazer flying as she pelted out through the house. No way was she going to leave Holly and Peter in there with those men!

She gave no thought to her aches and bruises as she dragged herself back over the garden fence.

Even as she bounced down into the garden, she saw Peter getting to his feet after his fall from the kitchen window.

'Peter!' she yelled. 'Where's Holly?'

Peter turned to look in through the open window. Water was still gushing from the broken pipes and Sparky was lying motionless under the cascade. But there was no sign of Holly.

'She's gone!' he cried. 'She was right behind me with Bruiser.'

The slamming of the front door echoed through the house.

Peter stared at Miranda in dismay. 'He must have caught her!' He heaved himself up on to the window-sill and jumped through the window, skidding and sliding as he sprinted across the kitchen floor.

He was in the hallway in a moment, dashing towards the front door. He jerked it open just in time to see the van pulling away from the kerb.

'Stop!' he yelled as he ran out on to the pavement. 'Somebody stop him!'

But there was no one to hear his shouts. The van gathered speed and swept away down the road.

Holly was in the passenger seat, clinging on for dear life as the big man drove recklessly along the road, spinning the wheel to make one screeching turn after another.

She glanced at the handle on the passenger door. She was no coward, but she knew it would be foolish to try and escape with the van going at such a speed.

'Where are you taking me?' she gasped as Bruiser's wild driving flung her from side to side.

'Shut up!' A heavy hand came out, pushing her down on to her side on the wide seat. 'Keep your head down and keep your mouth shut!'

She could no longer see where they were going. All she was aware of was the violent rattling of the van, and the stomach-turning swerves as they raced through the streets. Then a few minutes later the van came to a sudden halt, its brakes screaming.

The engine cut out. In the sudden quiet Holly could hear the panting of Bruiser's breath. She lifted her head. They had stopped in a narrow cul-de-sac. Brick walls reared all round her.

'Come on,' said Bruiser, shoving the driver's door open and catching hold of her collar.

121

It was all Holly could do to keep on her feet as he pulled her out of the van and dragged her towards a doorway set into the side wall.

'Let me go!' she gasped. 'You're hurting me!'

But Bruiser's grip was as hard as ever as he pushed the door open and thrust her through.

The door slammed behind them. They were in some kind of storeroom. Heavy metal shelves were filled with all kinds of electrical goods, and there were boxes piled everywhere.

'Keep quiet and you won't come to any harm,' said Bruiser. 'One word out of you and you'll be sorry.'

Holly nodded, swallowing hard.

I'll be all right, she said to herself. *Peter and Miranda will call the police.* But what help would *that* be? How long would it take them to find out where Bruiser had taken her?

Holly preferred not to think about that.

Bruiser led her to another doorway. He listened for a moment before opening the door a fraction.

'Gary!' he called. 'In here!'

The man called Gary came through.

'That was quick,' he began. 'You can put the stuff . . .' His voice trailed off as he saw Holly.

'I need some money,' said Bruiser.

'Who's *she*?' gasped Gary. He stared at Bruiser. 'What's going *on*?'

'We caught her nosing about in the house,' said Bruiser. 'Her and some other kids.'

'Where's Grant?' asked Gary.

'I don't know, and I don't care,' growled Bruiser. 'We've had it, you fool! The other kids will call the police. I'm going to get as far away from here as I can. And she's coming with me. The police won't try and stop me if they know I've got her on board.'

Holly saw the panic in Gary's face. 'What about *me*?' he gasped. 'They'll trace the stuff here.'

'That's your problem,' snarled Bruiser. 'Money! Now!'

'I – I'll get it from the till,' stammered Gary. He gave Holly a final frantic glance as he ran from the room.

'Where are you going to take me?' asked Holly, her brain racing. But Bruiser remained silent.

123

The door burst open and Gary came back in. He had a wad of bank-notes in his hand.

'This is all I could find,' he said. 'Let's get out of here.'

Bruiser snatched the money out of his hand. 'You're not coming with me,' he said.

'You've got to take me!' cried Gary. 'You can't just leave me.' He snatched at Bruiser's arm, but the big man shook him off.

'No way!' he said, pulling Holly towards the back entrance.

Gary let out a shout and jumped at the big man. With an angry grunt, Bruiser elbowed him away. Gary stumbled over backwards, crashing into a stack of cardboard boxes.

Now! thought Holly. She twisted in Bruiser's grip and felt his fingers slip away from her collar.

She ran to the door and caught hold of the handle. But Bruiser was on her in a second. His hand closed round her wrist and he wrenched the door open.

'No more tricks,' he growled. 'Get in the van.'

Her heart beating fast and her legs shaking, Holly climbed into the van. Escape now seemed impossible.

Two police cars came roaring up to the empty house on Roseway Road. No more than five minutes had elapsed since Miranda's phone call. Old Mr Frazer was out on the pavement with Peter and Miranda. They had done their best to explain to him what had happened, but they were both too panicky for anything they said to make much sense.

Miranda ran forwards as the police officers got out of the cars.

'They've taken our friend!' she shouted. 'You've got to do something! They've taken her off in the van.'

'Calm down,' said one of the officers, taking Miranda by the shoulders. 'Tell me exactly what's happened. Did you disturb burglars?'

'Yes! No!' babbled Miranda. 'They weren't burglars – I mean, they *were* burglars, but they weren't—'

'This place is full of stolen stuff,' interrupted Peter. 'And there's one of them in there.' He pointed towards the open front door. 'I think he's unconscious. But the other one has taken Holly. In a van. A blue van with "Drip-Busters!" written on the side. They were pretending to be plumbers. Miranda? What was the number of the van?'

'I don't remember,' wailed Miranda. 'Holly had it written down.'

'Go and check in there,' said the police officer to the others. He looked at Mr Frazer. 'Can you tell me what happened?'

'He doesn't know anything,' said Miranda. 'Please! You've got to get after the van.'

The officer spoke into his shoulder transmitter. 'We're at the scene,' he said. 'I'm not sure what's happened, but it looks like a girl has been taken hostage.' He gave Peter's description of the van. A voice crackled back.

'OK,' said the police officer. 'I'll get all the details I can from this end.'

'We've told you everything!' said Miranda.

'He's unconscious, all right,' shouted a policeman from the doorway of the house. 'There's water everywhere. It looks like there's been a real battle in here.'

'How many men were there?' asked the first officer. 'Could you describe them?'

'There were three of them,' said Peter.

'*Two*,' said Miranda. 'A big, grey-haired man and a younger one with dark-brown hair. They were wearing overalls – grey overalls.'

'There were three altogether,' said Peter. 'The third one was called Gary – but he wasn't with them the second time.'

The police officer stared at him. 'The *second* time?' he said. 'What do you mean?'

'There isn't time to explain,' said Peter. 'But there *were* three of them, and – *oh*!' His face suddenly lit up. 'I've got it!' He grabbed Miranda's arm. 'I've *got* it! I know where I've seen that man before! I just remembered!'

12 You can't win them all

Holly squeezed herself into the corner of the seat, trying to keep as far away from Bruiser as possible. He slammed the van door closed and started the engine. Things were happening so fast, she could hardly think.

The big man was sweating heavily as he jerked at the gear lever and swung the wheel. The van jumped forwards and there was a loud bang as the front bumper hit the wall of the narrow alley. Holly was thrown forwards.

With a snarl, Bruiser wrenched the gear lever back and turned the wheel again, sending the van careering backwards. There was another bang and a scraping noise as the rear of the van collided with the other wall.

Holly could see the panic on his face. At this rate the van would be wrecked before he got it out of the alley.

He muttered a curse and shoved the door open, leaning out to see what damage had been done in his frantic efforts to drive clear.

Holly looked at the ignition keys dangling from the steering block. She only had a second to act. She snatched at the keys and twisted them out of the ignition. She yanked the door handle down with her other hand and threw her full weight against the door. She tumbled out of the van, scrambled to her feet and ran.

The mouth of the alley was only a few metres away. Holly came pelting out into the street, gasping for breath. She recognised the street immediately. The row of shops. The empty area where the Sunday street market was held.

She was in Croftleigh Road. And the shop that stood alongside the alley was the second-hand shop where Peter had bought his video!

She ran out into the road and screamed at the top of her voice.

'Help!'

People in the street turned to stare at her and a couple of people ran towards her.

Bruiser was at the mouth of the alley, looking like a wild animal at bay as he saw the people running towards Holly.

Before Holly had time to gather her breath again, the whooping of police sirens filled the air. A police car came hurtling round the corner, screeching to a halt only a couple of metres from where she was standing.

She let out a yell of joy as she saw Bruiser turn and run.

But he didn't get far. Two police officers ran after him into the alley and brought him down.

A third policeman ran over to Holly.

'It's OK,' he said. 'You're safe now.'

'What about the others?' said Holly. 'Are *they* all right?'

A second police car rounded the corner and stopped behind the first one.

A back door burst open and Holly saw Miranda's relieved face as she climbed out.

'We got 'em!' yelled Miranda. 'We got *all* of them!'

The Mystery Kids were in Peter's house later that evening. Mr Hamilton sat on the sofa while the three friends sat in a ring on the floor to count up their car-washing money.

'Not bad,' said Holly, looking at the neat piles of coins. 'Not bad for a couple of days' work. Three burglars *and* all this money.'

All in all, it had been a very successful day. They had all given interviews to the police that afternoon. The raid on Square Deal had caught Gary, and a brief search in the back of the shop had uncovered the rest of the stolen stuff.

Mr Hamilton shook his head. 'I just wish you'd told me what you were doing,' he said. 'You could have got yourselves into a lot of trouble.'

'We didn't know it was burglars,' explained Holly. 'If we'd known *that*, we'd have told someone.'

'So what exactly were you doing in that house?' Mr Hamilton asked.

The three friends looked at one another. This was going to be quite a lengthy explanation.

They were saved by the doorbell.

'You can tell me all about it in a minute,' said Mr Hamilton. He smiled and shook his head. 'Although whether I'm going to understand it, is another matter.' He got up and went to answer the door.

'It was a good job I remembered where I'd seen Gary before,' said Peter. 'Fancy us buying our video from the shop where all the stolen stuff was being kept. And Gary actually served us!'

'You'd have saved us a lot of trouble if you'd remembered that a bit earlier,' said Miranda.

'It was the baseball cap,' said Peter. 'I couldn't see him properly. Anyway, I remembered in time, didn't I? They were all caught.'

Miranda giggled. 'Poor old Sparky,' she said. 'I bet he had a headache when he came round.'

'It serves him right,' said Holly. 'It serves all of them right.' She grinned. 'People should know better than to tangle with the Mystery Kids.'

'Does anyone fancy watching a video?' said Peter. 'I've hired a good one.' He put a video in the machine and pressed the remote control.

'Yess!' Holly and Miranda chorused as the credits rolled. It was their favourite TV programme, *Spyglass*.

'I didn't even know it was on video,' said Holly as she settled down to watch.

'It's only just come out,' said Peter.

They had hardly got past the opening titles when Mr Hamilton came back in, his face grim. A policewoman followed him into the room.

'Hello,' said Miranda. 'What now?' Her face lit up. 'I know,' she said. 'There's a reward! Is that it?'

'I'm afraid not,' said the policewoman. 'We have reason to believe that your video is stolen property.' She looked at Mr Hamilton. 'You did buy it from the shop called Square Deal in Croftleigh Road, didn't you, sir?'

'Yes,' said Mr Hamilton. 'I'm afraid I did. Peter, it doesn't look like we'll be watching anything this evening. I think the police want our video.'

'I'm afraid so,' said the policewoman. 'I'm very sorry about this.'

The video was disconnected and the policewoman took it away.

'What a rotten trick!' said Peter as the three friends sat staring at the space where the video recorder had been. 'And after all we've done!'

'Oh well,' Holly said with a rueful smile. 'You can't win them all. And we did catch the burglars, didn't we?'

Mr Hamilton came back into the room.

'Will you get your money back, Dad?' asked Peter.

'I don't know,' said Mr Hamilton. 'She said they'd be in touch.' He looked at the unhappy faces of the three friends. 'Don't worry about it,' he said. 'It's not the end of the world. It'll teach me to be a bit more careful about who I buy second-hand videos from in future.'

'So,' sighed Miranda. 'What now?'

Holly picked up the *Spyglass* video. 'I suppose we could watch it at my house,' she said.

Peter looked at his father. 'Would that be OK?' he asked.

Mr Hamilton smiled. 'Of course it would. Off you go. Although, considering the things you three get up to, I'm surprised you need to watch programmes about secret agents!'

Holly laughed. 'It gives us all sorts of new ideas for catching criminals,' she said.

'I think you've caught enough crooks for

one day,' said Mr Hamilton. 'Don't get involved in anything else, please!'

'Of course we won't,' said Holly. 'What could possibly happen between here and my house?'

'With you?' Miranda said, laughing. 'Anything!'

Another Hodder Children's book

Fiona Kelly

SMUGGLERS BAY
THE MYSTERY KIDS 5

Who knows the secret of Greystones house?

The Mystery Kids are in Cornwall
– the home of smugglers! They're
staying at Greystones, the imposing
old house of Mr Allenbury – and
Miranda is convinced that *he* is a
smuggler!

But then his young daughter, Lucy,
disappears . . .

Another Hodder Children's book

Fiona Kelly

FUNNY MONEY
THE MYSTERY KIDS 6

Can the Mystery Kids stop a forgery plot?

What is Peter doing with a fake ten pound note? He must have got it at the school car boot sale – but who would have given it to him?

The Mystery Kids do a little spying – and uncover an incredible secret plan . . .

THE MYSTERY KIDS SERIES
Fiona Kelly